DREAM'S LIFE

BY

ASSA RAYMOND BAKER

Acknowledgements

All praise be to God! This is for all of you who have been marching these years down with me so far and all of you that believe in my work. Thanks to G2G for giving me a chance and bringing this dream of mine to life in print. I have too many family and friends to list, so to all of you I send my love and prayers. And to all my haters, I'm still standing!

Forward

The smoke gray Ford Crown Vic pulled over, so Sam ran out. Once he jumped the fence surrounding the backyard of Nessa Heart's Childcare, the car sped off down the block and let out its last two passengers before the Little rounded the corner, pulled over, and turned out the headlights.

The last two men walked past the car in the direction of their intended victims. Mike casually sat on the hood of his rental, smoking a Black & Mild as he waited for his guy and the kid they came to pick up.

The streetlight reflected off of the wild-looking youngster's gold .45 that he pulled from his belt. This caught the man's eye just in time to see E-Bay take aim his way. He pulled his gun and sent shots at them first and then ducked down in front of the SUV. Before they could react, five shots hit home, dropping the youngster with the .45 as the other one dove behind a parked car.

"Folks! Folks! You good?"

When he didn't get an answer, Tay ran out from behind the car he was using for cover and fired wildly, trying to make it to his friend who was alive but knocked out cold.

The other guy returned fire as he jumped into the rental and pulled off, leaving the guy and the child behind.

"Fuck this shit! I ain't getting killed for nobody. I'm gonna take my black ass home!" Mike said out loud to himself.

Once he slowed to a stop at the light, he picked up his last Black & Mild from the floor. A car pulled up next to him with its windows down. He looked at it, but before he could react, the driver of the Crown Vic emptied his clip into the SUV and sped off. As the driver fought to hold on to his life, his foot slipped off of the break, and the Jeep slowly rolled in front of a passing city bus.

Happy with his job, the driver of the Crown Vic went back to the daycare to collect his people and get the one to the hospital or somewhere for help.

Table of Contents

Chapter 1

Enough Is Enough

From the outside, the immaculate mansion surrounded by armed guards looked safe and secure. But on the inside, Dream looked around her once beautifully decorated bedroom, which was now destroyed by her hands.

"Life is not this cell. I got to get away from this hell. I'm nobody's plaything. Who is he to treat people like they ain't shit? Fuck Him!" she said out loud to no one, before throwing a pillow from her bed.

Her best friend, Leslie, once told her to think of good things and better times when she got depressed. She said it was the best way to get through bad situations.

Dream pulled the comforter tightly around herself and prayed that Low Key received her message.

"Stop feeling sorry for yourself. Get up and move!" something inside her mind screamed at her.

Dream got out of the oversized bed and started planning her escape from the loveless prison that she once thought of as home to her and her seven-year-old daughter.

After the fall of the cartel, Cheez was the new big man in Miami. The drug trade circle there had been broken up into several groups, which was much smarter and safer for the Gomez Cartel that ran things straight out of Mexico.

"He got so much paper he can cash out almost anybody," Dice explained.

"It sounds a little suspect that ol' girl asked Low for help. I mean, why him?"

"It's not suspect to me. Low don't like the nigga Cheez since he had the Mexicans raise the prices in the northern states to better line his pockets. Every nigga getting real money in the streets knows that shit. So Low would be the best choice for her with all the money and power he got."

He paused.

"I hope she's for real about letting us get at him."

Dice got up and passed the unlit blunt.

Trigga accepted it, glanced at the television, and then asked, "Is he trying to pay me to do this, because I ain't heard shit about that part yet, my nigga."

"You got money, nigga. Do it on GP."

"Fam, you sound stupid right now! He yo' guy, not mine. I don't get down like that really no more, and you want me to do it on GP. That's fucking ridiculous!"

Dice laughed, half chocking on the last of the blunt he had been puffing on.

"Trigg man. I need you to do this for me or with me. I got a wife and kids to take care of now, and Low going to drop my prices and toss me some work so I can get my weight up in these streets. I wouldn't come at you on no bullshit."

"Sound good, my nigga, but it's too easy still. I think it's a setup or some shit to get you guys off his shit."

Trigga took a sip of his sweet tea.

"I'ma think hard on it. I know this bitch better be a bad muthafucka if I do go."

* * *

3

It was time for Dream to make her move if she truly wanted to be free of her predicament. She filled her daughter's book bag with as much money as she could, and then put the rest of the money and drugs from the floor safe in a backpack of her own. Cheez was in Mexico on one of his many business trips and wasn't expected back for a few days. Before he left, he put guards with her at all times, because he knew she was up to something.

As always, one of his goons, named Scotty, drove her to take Rahji to school. Dream went inside unescorted, where her best friend was waiting to sneak Rahji away along with the bags of drugs and cash.

Dream had called and informed the school that Rahji had a doctor's appointment so she wouldn't be in school that day. She then promised her friend that she would meet up with them as soon as she could before going back out to the awaiting car.

She knew how to use her good looks well. She also knew by the way Scotty was gawking at her in her skin-tight jeans and fitted low-cut shirt, which showed off her very shapely body, that she had him where she needed him to be. Plus, Dream had been giving him peep shows every night for almost a week. She would undress in front of her open bedroom window knowing he was watching her. She would even leave the bathroom door slightly open when she got in the shower so he could see her pleasure herself as she washed.

Now at home, Dream blocked what she was doing, and about to do, out of her mind. She tried to think of happy thoughts as Scotty plunged his hardness in and out of her over and over.

"Yes, oh yes! Get this pussy, daddy. I'm cumming. Ohhh God!"

She fucked him to send the fool over the edge. Scotty's eyes rolled back as he busted his nut. And in his moment of weakness, she lunged upward with both of her hands twisting his head until she heard his skinny neck break. She then jumped to her feet, scrambled to get dressed, and then covered the lifeless body on the bed, before she took his cash and car keys and ran out the door.

* * *

"Repeat what you just said to me, so I can be sure I heard you right!" Cheez called out as he held his cell phone so tight in his anger that you could hear the hard plastic crack.

"I—I said Dream killed Scotty. She took what was in your safe and ran off with your daughter."

"Bitch! You put that goofy-ass nigga on her instead of any other muthafuckin' body else?" Cheez snapped.

"He was the only one of us who don't really got shit to do but sit around and play PS3 all day."

But what Crunch didn't tell Cheez was that Scotty was found naked in his bed. He didn't want to be the next to die. Crunch knew it was best to let someone else be the fool.

"Find her!"

"I'm already on it. I got men out there looking right now. She won't get far."

"Dumb-ass nigga! She got enough money from that safe to hide any fucking where she wants!" he said, ending the call.

Cheez told Crunch to keep an eye on her because he felt Dream was going to leave after the beating he put on her before he left the house. Had Cheez not had to meet with the Gomez family, this never would have happened.

Cheez walked over and straightened himself up in the mirror.

"Two more days! Just two more! Then I'm going to find and bring my bitch back home," Cheez told himself in the mirror.

Chapter 2

What Friends Are For

Trigga stared at Dice for a minute.

"You might not need me now that you know she got out on her own."

"Nigga, is you mad? Tell me, is you mad? Tell me, is you mad because she got away all by herself?"

"Ain't nobody mad!" Trigga said as he took a sip of his bottled water. "I just don't see why I still need to be here."

"Yep, you mad!" Dice teased his friend. "You the same nigga who didn't want to do this in the first place!" Dice said smiling. "I still need you, Trig! I got to get her to the city safe, my nigga."

"Shit! We here now."

They posted up at the address that Low Key gave them in east Miami. This was where she said she would meet him. They weren't supposed to be there until two days from now, but Trigga wanted to be there way before she arrived just to be on the safe side. They found the safest rooms and bedded down for the wait.

"I'm out this bitch if she don't show up by tomorrow at this time, Dice; and you owe me for this shit too, fam!" Trigga said while pulling down his black Milwaukee fitted cap over his eyes.

"You got that, fam! When we get back home, I got you. You know if I owe you, you will never be broke," Dice responded jokingly, following Trigga's lead and doing the same with his New York cap.

* * *

Dice was awakened by the sound of tussling. Trigga was gone from the spot where he last saw him. He jumped to his feet and was met in the hall by his man Corn as they ran toward the sound. They saw two people struggling when they looked outside the kitchen window. Trigga was on top, but his gun was lying in the driveway a few feet away. The sound of the door opening caused

Trigga to take his eyes off of the person with whom he was struggling. He then caught one in the face.

The first hit brushed his chin and dazed him. The other person then took advantage of this and broke toward the gun. Dice snatched the gun up off the ground. Trigga used the distraction to knock his wild opponent out.

"Man, this bitch is fast. She almost got me," Trigga said as he stood up.

"That's a bitch you was fighting with?" Corn asked in shock.

"Are you sure that's a female?" Dice followed up.

"What the fuck! Yeah, I know the difference!"

Dice and Corn then walked up on her. She was dressed in dark colors, and her face was shadowed by the dark.

"Your hands got blood on them," Dice told his boy.

Trigga looked down at his hands.

"It's not mine. It must be hers."

He kneeled down and pulled up her shirt.

"Is it bad?" Dice asked.

"It's hard to see out here. Help me get her in the house so I can try to stop the bleeding. We don't need her to die on us!" Trigga explained.

Once in the house, Corn found a needle and thread as Trigga did his best to stitch her up while the others held her down just in case she woke up fighting before he finished.

"Where did you learn how to do that?"

"From this army nigga I was in the Feds with. I told you niggas I know a little bit of everything!"

* * *

Back at the mansion, one of the men found dry blood on the iron gate that surrounded the grounds. They had informed Crunch, so he and Cheez followed him to the spot where he found the blood.

"She must've hurt herself when she climbed over," Crunch suggested.

"Fool-ass nigga! If she climbed over the gate, why is the car missing?" Cheez interjected.

Cheez turned and walked back toward the house.

"She did this shit to throw us off!"

Crunch touched the blood with his bare hand.

"I think she's hurt for real. Go look for her! Take two more niggas with you and find that bitch!" he ordered the guards.

"Since you so sure, nigga, you go with them and check out the hospital. And if you can't find her there, go to that bitch Leslie's house. She's the only muthafuckin' person she got to run to here."

Cheez smiled at his thought and ordered them to split up and look in both places. Although he knew how smart she was, it wouldn't be too easy for her to run with Rahji with her. She would need help, and Leslie would be just the person to whom she would turn.

* * *

Dream tried to stand up but fell back down.

She looked at Dice and asked, "Which one of you hit me?"

"You swung at me first, and you tried to kill me. I didn't have a choice!" Trigga said in his defense.

"Can you help me up, please?" she asked Dice.

Dice then pulled her to her feet. She held on to him tightly to keep from falling.

"I ain't never seen you before, plus didn't nobody know I was coming here. So, y'all must be with Low Key."

"Yeah. He sent us to bring you to him. So what up?" Corn asked.

"Where do we go from here?" Trigga joined in.

Dream didn't even look at him when she replied, informing him she would tell them when they got there.

"Whatever! Put her in the front seat, Corn. I'm driving. Fam, knock her ass out if she try something else!" Trigga called out as he quickly jumped in the rented SUV.

"Go straight and then make a left as soon as you can," Dream explained, before she turned to Dice, who was seated behind Trigga. "How do I know he's not working for Cheez? He acts just like one of his fake-ass goons!" Dream said as if Trigga wasn't right next to her driving the vehicle.

"I know him. So you just going to have to trust in me that I made a good choice in bringing him with me to come get you. Plus, any one of us would've done the same, because we wasn't looking for you to show up until the next day."

Dream rolled her eyes and turned back around.

They continued to drive in silence for miles; however, after crossing a bridge, Dream finally spoke up.

"Turn left at the stop sign."

"I thought you was asleep."

"That's what you get for thinking!" she answered. "I don't talk to you, so please don't say shit to me!" she said smartly to Trigga.

Dream was mad that he had hit her, so she couldn't deal with him. She wished Dice had not brought him.

She prayed he hadn't been paid off by Cheez. If he had been, she wouldn't think twice about doing what she had to do for herself and her child. She only trusted Dice because she had heard of him, but she didn't know anything about the other two.

"That's the house over there! Pull 'round back!"

Chapter 3

Hidden Treasure

Trigga put the truck in park and pulled his gun on Dream. Her heart almost stopped.

"I don't think so. Who in this house?" he questioned her, stopping her from getting out of the truck.

"What?"

"Here! Cell them and tell 'em to step out with their hands up so we can see them," Corn told her as he handed her his phone.

She did as she was told, and moments later the door opened and a woman called out to her. Dream jumped from the truck.

"I was worried about you!" Leslie said before hugging her. "Who are they?" she continued as she looked back at the SUV.

"They safe. They're going to get us out of here."

Dice led the pack over to them. Trigga had his eye open for anything, and his finger on the trigger. He was ready to handle whatever came their way.

Once they were all inside the house and introductions were made, Leslie got everyone something cold to drink.

"Don't worry, nigga. I got it here."

"I believe you're supposed to be giving us something for Low."

"Sorry! I'm from the Show Me State. So I'ma need that before we can do anything else!" Trigga said.

Dream turned to Dice and told him to follow her, knowing that Trigga spoke for the both of them. She told them to be quiet when they reached the closed bedroom door.

"There she is, and I'll give you the list in the morning when you get us all out of here," Dream explained.

"I don't understand. Who is she?"

"Her name is Rahji, and she's Cheez's daughter."

"You kidnapped his little girl?" Trigga asked, confused.

16

"No. She's our child! He didn't know about her until three years ago. That's when I thought things would be better for me with him, but I was wrong. They was worse, at least for me. It was hell in that house!" Dream told him before she walked them back through the house.

"He has a wife, and two kids with her, but after her last birth, something went wrong. That baby died, and now she can't have no more kids. So he's going to come looking for us. I know I said I would give you this in the morning, but here."

Dream then handed Dice a black journal.

"I also took some keys of dope, but that's the list of all the people he deals with. It has everyone who's anyone in it."

Dream didn't tell them about the money she also took. That was her safety net in case they got on something.

"I'm not asking for nothing but for y'all to get us away from him. I know he will come after us, and that's how y'all can catch him slipping."

"And kill his punk ass!" Leslie butted in from her seat in the living room.

Trigga sat down and thought about what was being said to him. He knew the journal was good to have, even for a guy like him who wasn't into the street life too much any longer. He also knew that if Low Key could kill Cheez, he would be the next man if he played his hand right. He looked around at the people around him and wondered if he wanted to see how this played itself out.

Leslie's light skin was honey-kissed and brought out her brown eyes. She was tall, and her Seven jeans and T-shirt hugged her body, giving off just a little bit but not too much sexiness.

"What?" she asked Trigga.

"What *what*?"

"You been studying me like I'm a test subject or some shit!"

"I'm just curious, but I don't want to offend you or be disrespectful in no way."

"Yes I am, and no we aren't!" she answered.

She knew his questioning was to find out if she was gay and if she and Dream were a couple.

"I met her down here in Miami when I was working strip clubs. It helped pay my way through school. She was working for some lame-ass, wanna-be pimp nigga from Chicago who got killed by one of his girls for one too many ass whippings. I took her in and put her under my wing, and the rest is for her to tell you. We are like sisters!"

Leslie then stood up to get them another beer.

"Why didn't she just leave and go somewhere else before all this bullshit or when she first saw it coming?" Trigga questioned.

"She had no money or no real way to care for herself or a baby, without doing the only thing she knew how. But she did her best. She fucked up by falling for Cheez's hoe ass. She thought he would leave his wife for her."

"So you believe that's Cheez's daughter?" Dice asked.

"I know she is. Just because a woman works in a strip club don't mean she's a hoe. Yes, many of them are, but not all. It's all the same in them cold streets. Some do what they wanna do, and others do what they gotta do!" Leslie further explained before she downed the rest of her beer.

Corn got up and excused himself. He told Trigga he was going to post up outside in the truck. He was a light sleeper and thought it would be best if he was outside just in case something jumped off. Leslie got up and locked the door behind him. She then returned to her spot and continued talking with Trigga and Dice.

After the little talk with Leslie, Trigga went in search of Dream. He found her in the back bedroom trying to re-dress herself. But she was having a difficult time because of her wounded side.

"Here! Let me help you," he offered.

"I don't need your help. Get out! Didn't I say not to talk to me earlier? Now get out!" she scolded him, before turning her back.

Trigga stood in the door way.

"Why didn't you call Leslie to help you?" he questioned, before helping her get dressed anyway.

"Because I'm good. I would've got it together on my own."

"Well, damn," he laughed. "Is she coming to the Chi with us?"

"Yeah. What you about to say? That she can't, or you don't want her to?"

"Baby girl, I'm just asking, that's all! Damn! We really need to start over if we going to be spending time together for the next day or so."

"So Dice is going to take us?"

"Probably so. He's a good-guy-ass nigga. Ain't that why you got up with Low Key, because you knew he would?"

"I called Low Key because I know he got the money and the power to keep us safe. He told me he would send Dice, so I trust him. I don't know shit about you, so I don't trust you," she told him smartly.

"Well, my nigga asked me to help him get your smart-mouth ass back to the Chi, and that's when my part in this soap shit ends."

Trigga then reached into his pocket and handed her a pack of Ibuprofen. He was smiling when he passed Leslie coming out of the bathroom.

"Hey, Les, see if you can get her to take the Ibuprofen I gave her, since she don't trust me and shit."

"Oh God! Okay. I'll see if I can. I may have something a little stronger than that over-the-counter stuff," Leslie said as she walked over toward Dream.

Trigga found Dice standing outside the back door smoking a blunt and talking on his cell phone.

"So, it sounds like you made up your mind," Trigga heard Dice say into the phone.

"I believe her. All my people say the nigga's going nuts looking for her," Low Key responded.

"But what if he just says 'fuck her' and gets a new bitch? Then what did I lose?" Dice questioned.

"Don't worry, my nigga. He needs that list, so I got you either way," Low Key assured him, before they ended the call.

Dice took the blunt back from Trigga.

"That was Low. He still wants us to bring her," Dice said.

"We been lucky so far. This has been too easy," Trigga said before he knocked on the wooden door for good luck.

"Niggas like Cheez think they shit don't stank. Like they run the world or something," Dice chimed.

"Hey, my nigga. I don't give a fuck. I'll get y'all back safe, and then I'm gone. Don't call me, nigga, never, ever, ever, ever again!" Trigga joked.

"By the way, Low rented us a plane so we won't get caught up on the highway and so we can get to the city faster. He said his people will pick us up from the airport and take us to the safe house," Dice explained before he smashed the finished blunt out on the ground.

"Okay! I'm still going to make sure you get there. Then I'm gone, my nigga!" Trigga reiterated.

Trigga and Dice waved at Corn, who flashed the lights to let them know he was on point. They both then walked back into the kitchen.

* * *

There was nothing more beautiful in the world than the sight of her sleeping beauty. Dream stood in the doorway of Rahji's room.

"Mama."

The sound of her daughter's little voice snapped Dream from her thoughts.

"Yes, baby girl? Mama didn't mean to wake you up. Go back to sleep."

"But I'm not sleepy," she lied.

"Girl, you better try. It's late!" Dream whispered as she stood right next to her daughter's bed.

"Can you sleep with me then?"

"Okay, but no more talking. Go back to sleep. We got a lot to do tomorrow."

Dream then crawled into bed with her daughter.

"I love you, Mama!"

Dream let out a little laugh.

"I love you too! Now goodnight."

Rahji put her arm around her mother and fell back to sleep immediately. Dream said a little prayer of thanks and asked the Lord to continue to keep them safe, before she too fell off to sleep.

Chapter 4

Do You Have to Go?

Have you found her yet?"

"No! But I found out where that bitch lives now!" Crunch paused as he pushed the white girl's head back down between his legs, letting her know to mind her own. "I'm sending niggas out there right now. I'll let you know as soon as I hear something else."

"No, I'm here! So I want to go with y'all to get my baby girl and kill that bitch myself," Cheez said into his cell.

Cheez drove his Range Rover from the small airport, followed by two matching SUVs, which would sometimes surround his.

Crunch jumped to his feet and knocked the poor girl off the bed. She hit the floor hard and bruised her arm.

"Okay, I'll meet you at the spot, and we can both ride out from there," Crunch replied to his boss.

Cheez agreed and then hung up the cell phone. He chirped the lead SUV and told the driver where to go. He then turned back up his homeboy Rick Ross's song and lit up some of Miami's finest kush.

* * *

Once Crunch arrived at the spot where Cheez waited for him, he told him that he just got a call informing him that Dream was heading toward the airport.

"Muthafuck! I was just at that bitch!" Cheez yelled as he and his men all raced to their trucks to try to cut them off.

"She got some people with her!" Crunch informed him.

"Who?"

"Roe say it's her, Leslie, and the baby for sure, but he thinks one of them is Low Key's guy," Crunch explained while driving Cheez's truck.

"Low Key? What the fuck's he got to do with this shit?" Cheez questioned as he pulled his gun out from its stash place, set it on his lap, and looked out the window.

"Yeah, he's the one who called and told me that Dream was on her way to the airport to Chicago with him."

"Why did he tell you all this?"

"He said you'd know what to do if you want her and your little black book back."

After getting Low Key's number from Crunch, Cheez called him himself.

"Low! What it do? What's this about, my nigga?"

"Hey! Yo' bitch called me and made me an offer I couldn't pass up. But gangsta to gangsta, I know we can work something out. I only talk money, feel me?"

"So let's talk numbers."

After making a deal to let him get his work for $12K per brick of pure flake if he sent Dream and her friends to his ranch in Georgia, Low Key placed a call to have them taken there instead of to Chicago where he was.

* * *

The pilot announced the change in flight plans over the intercom. Dice then informed everyone of Low Key's change in plans to have them put up at his house in Savannah, Georgia. It was hard, but Dream talked Leslie into leaving everything behind that she had worked so hard for and to start over with her and Rahji. She promised to split the money that she had taken from the safe down the middle with her.

Leslie was sold on the idea of having over $350K to do with as she liked.

Dream didn't trust having too many people know where she would be located, but she also knew she would have to let Dice do what Low Key ordered him to do in order to be safe from her past.

"Do you know any of these niggas that will be picking us up from the airport?" she asked, wondering why she still didn't feel safe.

"I know Low, so I don't need to know his niggas!" Dice answered with confidence.

"Well, I'm responsible for my baby and my sister, so it's going to be hard for me to trust anyone. I told you before that Cheez got people everywhere."

Dream knew she would never be safe until Cheez was dead, because he could still have her touched from inside a prison cell with all his money and power.

"It's just as important to me to get Cheez," Dice told her.

"Is Trig coming with us?" she asked, looking at him and Leslie talking to each other while holding her sleeping princess.

She was getting kind of comfortable with the way he took charge.

Dice hesitated, since he did not want to turn her off with the change in plans that came at the last minute from Low Key.

"I was lucky he came in the first place, so I don't know for sure. But he's told me more than once that he's gone once he gets us to where we need to be. But maybe he might, if you asked him to stay," Dice said with a laugh.

"What the fuck ever!" Dream smiled, knowing Dice had picked up on her change of heart about Trigga. "You seeing shit, nigga. I just want him to make sure we cool, and I feel he knows how to do just that.

Chapter 5

Money Over You

Trigga felt her eyes before he even turned to meet them. He sensed the call for help in Dream's eyes, but Trigga didn't know if he wanted to be involved any farther than he had already. He had put in his time in the streets. And he wasn't in a hurry to get back to them. He did sometimes miss the excitement, but that's why he was here now.

Trigga made his money doing hits when he was a teenager. As he got older, drugs got thrown into the mix of how he planned to get his family out of the ghetto. His mind drifted to the day that he made that transformation from skilled hit man to drug dealer.

* * *

He was only eighteen years old, but he had been doing hits already for five years. The date was June 16, 2003. He and his girlfriend at the time, Megan, were hanging out poolside at Coolwater Water Park when he got the· call from Assa.

"What up?" Trigga answered as he stepped away from Megan.

"What up with you?"

"Shit, trying to stay cool!" Trigga replied with a smile while looking over at Megan's brother dunking her in the pool.

"I hear that. But tell me, is you working, or is this a play day?"

"I'm always on call, boss man. You should know that by now."

"Right! Right! Well, come see me as soon as you get free."

"Fo' sho'," Trigga replied before he hung up.

He told Megan he had something to do that had just come up, so he would have to get up with her later. She was used to him running off on her, but for some reason, today she wasn't going to hear it.

"Trigga, if you leave me today, you may as well stay wherever it is you about to run off to," she said while rolling her eyes. "If you go, you may as well keep on going. I ain't playing."

That was the last time Trigga saw Megan as his girlfriend.

* * *

He met up with Assa and got the name and address, and the $5,000 that he charged for the job. Trigga didn't even go home and change; he just went. Trigga was always strapped, so he made himself comfortable as he waited for Black Bill to show up. He was glad the parking garage gave him some shade from the beaming sun.

Four hours later, Black Bill's Range Rover entered the garage. Trigga followed him to the sixth level, where Black slid his truck into its spot. Trigga drove past him, found a spot, grabbed his Hi-Point .45, and ran to catch the keycard door to the stairs before it closed. Bill heard Trigga's footsteps, but when he turned to look, he didn't see anybody. So he dismissed it as his echo and kept walking.

But something told Bill to look back over his shoulder. As he did, it was just in time to see Trigga fire his first shot. Bill ducked, and the shot missed his head. He ran down the steps two and three at a time as fast as his forty-seven-year-old legs would move his 270 pounds.

But Trigga was younger and faster. He shot for the second time. But this time his shot hit Black Bill in the upper back, sending him crashing into the wall.

"Please don't kill me, man! Please don't! Just take it! Take it all!"

Bill cried like a baby.

"I'll give you whatever you want. There's fifty grand and twelve keys in there. It's yours! Just please don't kill me!" he begged.

"Sorry, my nigga. I got to do what I got to do. Plus, you made me run on a hot-ass day like this, and I think I lost my bitch because of yo' hoe ass."

He pointed the .45 in Black Bill's face and pulled the trigger. He then picked up the blue duffle bag, ran back to his Regal, and never looked back after that day.

* * *

He put money in all the right places, so now he was set for life. He knew he didn't have to do this, but Trigga felt he was missing something. Now that it was time for them to go their separate ways, he felt the need to make sure Dream got to where she was going.

"Dice and Low's goons could finish this job," he told himself as he walked into the airport to get the next flight out.

But after learning that the next flight to Milwaukee wasn't until morning, he decided to make a few calls for his own curiosity.

Chapter 6

Let Me Do Something

Dice, I want a gun, and I don't want none of them other niggas in here around my baby. I'm only going to let you and Corn get close to any of us," Dream announced.

"Do you know how to use a gun?"

"I know how to use a gun, my hands, my feet, and whatever else I have to use to survive," Dream replied.

Dice simply shook his head.

"Here! Take one of mine. I always stay double-heated," he explained as they walked into the house.

Dice then introduced Dream and Leslie to the six men who were sent to watch them.

* * *

The next day passed by pretty fast. They all just enjoyed the warm summer breeze.

Rahji and Corn sat down and played War Lord II on the PS3 while Dream sipped a beer as she watched them from across the room.

"What's on your mind?" Dice asked her while rolling up a blunt.

"Being in that house with him was like a prison. My baby has never been to the zoo or out to a movie. I bet he did all that and more with his wife and her kids," Dream began as she took another sip. "I feel my baby's been cheated out of so much, and I'm going to make it all up to her and myself when this is over."

Dream quietly sat thinking about the money she had.

"Don't beat yourself up. You did what you had to, just like you're doing now," he said while lighting his blunt.

"When is Low coming?"

"That nigga said he will be here. He's got a bunch of shit to do now that you put Cheez in his reach," Dice answered as he blew out the sweet smoke.

"Well, I just hope he hurry up!"

Dream got up and went into the kitchen, where she found Leslie cooking and dressed in sweats and a T-shirt.

"Hey, girl!"

"Hey! I figured everybody would be about ready to eat something, so I'm about to fry this chicken and make some fries," Leslie said.

"Do you want me to help?" Dream asked as she began to wash her hands.

"Hell yeah! You can start cutting the fries, or do you want to cut and clean this bird?" she asked, holding a whole chicken in her hand by its leg.

"No, you go 'head and handle that," she responded as they both laughed.

While Leslie told her what she thought about everything, Dream found herself thinking about Trigga. Although she truly felt safe when he was around, she would have to get used to living like this, she thought as she cut the potatoes.

Chapter 7

You Missed a Spot

Crunch sat in his Benz S550 talking on his cell in Cheez's driveway.

A few minutes later, Cheez pulled up and parked next to him, got out, and walked toward his house.

Crunch ended his call and fell in step right behind him.

"Everybody is ready and are where they're supposed to be. Oh, and just so you know, I still charged Low Key full price this round. I told the nigga it was the last, and we'll start with the new numbers when the re comes in."

"Okay, I want you to make time to deal with that rat-ass nigga. If he would sell them out to us, you know what he would do if the people got a hold of him."

Cheez spotted his daughter peeking around the corner at him. This was a game they played every day.

"Did you find out who the other nigga was with her?" Cheez asked as he scooped up his daughter.

"No, but one of them ain't with them no more. He broke off at the airport."

"I still want to know who the fuck he is. If you can't do what the fuck is asked of you, find me somebody who can, and kill yourself!" Cheez snapped.

Crunch assured Cheez that he could handle this, and he thought Cheez would be pleased that he got them at the ranch surrounded by his men. They were told to play the role until they were told otherwise.

Crunch looked at his white gold, iced-out watch. It was time for him to go to the gym. He worked out hard four days a week to keep his 260 pounds solid. He was a big, beefy, dark-skinned, short man around five foot seven. He wore his hair in long dreads. He was the closest person to Cheez outside of his wife and kids. Even though he wouldn't say it, Crunch knew Cheez would never replace him.

When he met Cheez, Crunch was fresh out of prison with nothing and nobody to lean on. His family had written him off long ago when he shot his little cousin for wearing his new shoes. He got a job at a carwash to keep something in his pockets.

One day, Cheez pulled into the carwash and offered Crunch a job as his personal bodyguard. Unbeknownst to him, Cheez had been testing him for the past week. Sometimes he would leave a wad of cash lying around. He would do this in different cars, and not one penny was ever missing.

Cheez didn't really need a bodyguard, since he was very skilled in karate. He just didn't like to use guns, and Crunch loved to, so they were a match made in hell.

Chapter 8

On My Way

Trigga sat in the airport's rental car office on the phone with one of his old friends, Monty. Monty told Trigga all he knew about what was going on with Cheez. After being told that Low Key went missing, Trigga felt the need to get back to them at the ranch.

"Tell me about the nigga named Crunch."

"He's Cheez's right hand. He calls the shots, or more like he passes the boss's word down and enforces it on the streets. He's as heartless as they come. The nigga won't think twice about who he kills," Monty explained.

Trigga didn't like the feeling he had. Low Key and Dice had hopes that Cheez would come after Dream himself. But it would make sense to send one of his goons to bring them to him and deal with her when they did.

He called Dice's number over and over, only to get his voice mail. He didn't know what he would tell them if he was just over-thinking things, but he wasn't going to take the chance on letting it go either.

Trigga removed his gun from its special carrying case that he had made for air travel. He then raced out toward the ranch, pushing the rental car way past the speed limit.

Chapter 9

The Ranch

Multiple gunshots echoed throughout the house. Dream dropped what she was doing, grabbed the gun that Dice had given her, and ran from the kitchen. Leslie was right behind her, armed with only the knife she was using.

Dream didn't ask any questions when she sent head shots at the man standing over Corn's body lying only a few feet from the game. He dropped dead. Rahji was nowhere in sight. They panicked and called her name as Leslie took Corn's gun from his lifeless hand.

"I'll look for her upstairs. You look down here, but don't go outside without me."

Dream had picked up the other man's gun and was out the front door before she could finish talking. Knowing she couldn't afford to stop her, Leslie continued upstairs to look for Rahji. She hoped she had gone to wash up for dinner like her mother had told her. Leslie called out Rahji's name, and relief flooded over her when the little girl came out of the bathroom crying.

"Tee-tee, I'm scared."

"It's okay, baby! It's okay. I'm going to need for you to stop crying so we can go get you mama."

Outside Dream felt someone grab her arm. She swung her gun back forcefully.

"Hey! Hey! Dream, it's me!" Trigga responded, blocking the deadly blow she aimed at his nose.

"Trigga? I knew I shouldn't have trusted you!"

He spun out of his hold and found himself standing there with his hands up.

"It's not me. I came back to help, but we can talk all that out later. Let's hurry up and find the others so we can get out of here."

He pushed her back toward the house.

"I know Crunch is on his way here, if he's not here somewhere already."

"Crunch? He sent his bitch ass?" Dream exclaimed.

They ran into Leslie, who was coming downstairs with Rahji.

"Close your eyes, baby, and don't open them until I tell you to, okay?"

"Okay!" Rahji answered Leslie, doing as she was told.

Leslie didn't want her to see the dead men as they passed.

Once Trigga had them all together, he asked them where Dice was. But no one knew. So he told them to run straight for the road where his rental was parked.

"If I don't show in ten minutes, drive to the airport."

They did as they were told as Trigga ran toward the sound of more gunshots, where he found Dice taking cover not far from a large propane tank.

Dice turned to the sound coming from behind him.

"Where you come from?" he smiled, when he saw his one-man reinforcement.

"Low is missing, but let's get out of here and talk about this. I got the girls already," Trigga explained.

"Alright, my nigga. We got to make it to the house and away from this thing," Dice suggested as he pointed to the tank.

"Follow me! On the count of three, get up shooting and break for the road. You'll see the girls in a car not far from the house if we get separated."

"Fo' sho'!" Dice agreed.

"One . . . two . . . three. Go!"

They jumped to their feet shooting and running. Dice shot at Cheez's men, but Trigga sent his shots into the propane tank. After his fifth and last shot, the tank exploded with such force that he and Dice were knocked off their feet and the house caught fire.

The girls ducked at the sound of the blast. Seconds later, they saw two shadowy figures running toward them.

"There they go, Ma!" Rahji said through her sobs.

"Here comes another car. Everybody duck!"

As they did, Dream looked from the rear-view mirror. The SUV passed them so fast that the car shook. It turned into the driveway to the ranch and stopped.

Crunch leaned out the passenger-side window and squeezed the trigger of his AK. A few feet in front of him, two men ran from the house fire. Knowing they were his target, he continued to fire rounds in their direction.

Trigga zig-zagged after seeing dirt jump at his feet from the missed shots. He turned his head, only to witness Dice's head explode. His body did a full flip before it hit the ground. Leslie covered Rahji's eyes and looked at Dream in shock at seeing Dice's murder.

"Did you see that?"

"I wish I didn't!" Dream answered.

She turned the car around and pointed it toward the highway.

Seeing the car moving made Trigga take off at a full-speed pace as hard as he could to catch it. The thick smoke from the burning house covered him as he ran. Crunch fired repeatedly into the smoke.

Shots slammed into the ground just as Trigga dove into the back seat of the car. Dream peeled off before he even had time to shut the door. No one spoke until they were safely on the highway.

"How's everybody? Ain't nobody hurt, right?" he asked, breaking the silence.

"No, I'm scared!" Rahji whispered while Leslie hugged her tighter.

He told them it was okay now and that he wouldn't let anything happen to them. They all prayed to God he was telling the truth.

"Where are we going?" Dream asked. "I don't know how to work the GPS," she admitted to him.

"Oh, pull over anywhere so I can drive."

Trigga got behind the wheel while still trying to catch his breath. He told them they were going to his house as he drove back toward the airport.

Chapter 10

Home Sweet Home

The house on East Clark and Mason was huge—not like Dream's mansion, but too big for one person. Its color theme was burgundy, gold, and beige. There were three full bathrooms and five bedrooms, which was certainly more than enough room for the four of them. Trigga told them to make themselves comfortable.

Leslie then carried the sleeping child into one of the bedrooms and laid her down. Dream walked in on her just as she was wiping tears from her face. They had been through too much in the last few days.

"Girl, you should see how nice this place is. It's not too big and not too small," Dream said, not wanting to tell her that she saw her daughter's tears. "I wanted to tuck

49

my baby girl in bed. I think Trigga's in the kitchen making coffee."

"Shit! I need a real drink!"

They shared a short laugh in agreement before Leslie left Dream to get undressed and tuck her child into bed. Dream then kissed Rahji's forehead.

"I love you, baby girl."

"I love you back, Mama," Rahji responded before rolling over and snoring softly.

Dream fluffed her pillow before walking out the door, leaving it cracked so she could hear Rahji if she needed her. She was met in the hallway by Leslie holding a glass and a gun.

Normally this would look strange, but not in these times.

"What's up?"

"All he had was tequila!" Leslie said with a smile, knowing it was Dream's favorite drink. "I'ma sleep in here with her just in case she wakes up or has nightmares or some shit."

"You need your rest too."

"I'm good. Go talk to Trigga and find out what's next for us." She pushed her down the hallway.

Dream took a deep breath.

"I'll be back to see 'bout y'all," she said before moving on.

Dream found Trigga in his living room listening to Kem, who filled the room with his soulful words of love and life.

Trigga asked her how Rahji was doing, and she told him she was okay and asleep.

"Can I ask you something?"

"Go 'head!"

She asked him what made him come back after telling them he was returning to Milwaukee. Trigga told her he had a feeling that something was wrong, so he made a few calls on the strength that he and Dice went back a few years. The thought of his lost friend made him take a drink.

"I just wanted to make sure things was cool. When I couldn't get Low on the phone, I decided to come back to be on the safe side."

"So you had a feeling and came back to warn us?" she confirmed.

"Yeah. But by the time I got there, all hell had broken loose already."

Dream was studying his face to see if she could read any traces of a lie.

"Thank you for coming back for us. I would pay you, but all our money was in the house when it blew up."

"Don't worry about that. I got y'all. Whatever y'all need, I got you. Just trust me a little, Dream."

"I do trust you. I honestly do!"

Chapter 11

I Can't Believe You

Dice and his men are dead. We lost a few of ours too."

"So you got that bitch and my shit?" Cheez asked, getting straight to the point.

"No, they got away!" Crunch hesitated. "But we'll have them soon," he told his boss, knowing Cheez was about to snap on him for not having them.

"Fuck you mean no!" he asked angrily.

Crunch explained to him everything that had gone down, from the shootout to the explosion.

"It was like they knew we were coming and were waiting on us or something."

"You fucked up somewhere!"

"I don't see how when they were surrounded by all our men. Dice and that lil' nigga were all they had with them, once that other nigga left," Crunch explained to him.

"How the fuck did they get away if Dice and the other guy were dead, and the other nigga was gone?" Cheez demanded.

"I don't know, but I'm working on it. A female at the airport I fucked with told me that two women, a little girl, and a man booked a flight to Wisconsin. It must be someone her friend knows."

"That bitch don't know fucking nobody in Wisconsin! I've been with her too long. She would've said something to me."

"Ol' girl said the computers had gone down, so she couldn't tell me exactly where in Wisconsin."

"Stand on the bitch at the airport. Buy the bitch a new car or something. If that don't work, start breaking shit on her body. Just get me what I need!"

Cheez hung up the phone on Crunch. He only had a few more days in Mexico to lock down the new deal with Mr. Gomez, and then he would be free to find Dream himself. He couldn't deal with the excuses too much longer. He took a deep breath like he had learned in his yoga classes, to tame his anger. After a moment or two he would be in control of his emotions again.

Cheez didn't want to rely on anybody to bring them back to him, but he had to.

"Money over everything!" he said out loud, shaking off thoughts of how good the sex was with Dream.

He thought it would be so good to fuck her once more before he killed her and then took his daughter back home so she could be with his other family where she belonged, in his mind. He walked back into the room where his wife was sitting and talking to her mother.

"Mrs. Gomez, can I steal my wife from you for a second?"

"Only if you call me Mom! You act like you're not a part of this family by calling me by my last name."

"Mama, I told you it's hard for him to do right. Now just give him time!" Amilia spoke up for her husband.

She again reminded her mother that Cheez grew up in a boy's school and never knew his mother or father. So he wasn't comfortable with calling anyone Mom or Dad."

Chapter 12

New Friends New Place

The next morning Dream looked in to find her princess still sleeping, but Leslie was no longer in the bed with her. She then wandered around the house until she ran into Trigga.

"This is a nice house you got. I wouldn't have pictured you living like this."

"Thanks, I guess!" he answered, punching in the alarm code to disarm it.

"Is it really yours?" she asked while looking at pictures on the walls.

"Yes, it belonged to my mother. May she rest in peace!"

"How did she pass, if you don't mind me asking?"

Trigga explained the story to Dream about when he lost his mother and sister in a bad car crash when they were coming to visit him while in prison. When he got out sixteen months later, he paid off the banknote and moved into the house he had bought for his mother. It made him feel closer to both of them.

Suddenly, a man dressed in black sweats and a wifebeater walked from the back of the house.

"Good morning, everybody," he greeted.

"Morning, fam," Trigga responded before quickly introducing him to Dream. "This is Paper. He's like my brother. You don't got to be worried about this nigga. He's a pussycat," Trigga joked.

"Fuck you! Show me I'm pussy, nigga! You lucky she's here."

The two men laughed as they playfully took swings at one another.

Paper lived in the lower level of the house. It was far from a basement. They had it remodeled into another apartment minus a kitchen, which they shared on the main level of the house. He was twenty-seven years old, and tall and muscular. His eyes were low and misty gray. His light skin made him a woman's dream.

"You must be Dream, because I ran into what's her name a few minutes ago."

"Leslie!" Dream reminded him.

"Yeah, that's her name!"

"Have you heard anything from or about Low Key yet?" Trigga asked.

"Nope, not yet. But I just got up, so let me check my voice mail."

"Mama, can I play with the doggy?" Rahji questioned while holding up the cutest little lap dog.

"I got two questions for you niggas," Leslie started while standing beside Rahji. "Just what kind of dog is this cute little ball of fun, and which one of you two thug-ass niggas does it belong to?"

Dream gave Rahji the okay to play with the dog, and then laughed at the two men for having it.

"It's mine. Her name is Tracy. She belonged to my sister," Trigga answered. "She's a mixed breed called a teddy bear, but she thinks she's a black bear sometimes."

"She won't bite her. I see the question in your face," Paper said to Dream as he walked by her to help with breakfast.

After the meal, Paper took Leslie to the Bayshore Mall to purchase the three of them a few items of clothing and personals to get them through a few days or until they made their next move.

Leslie couldn't believe how much fun she was having just being around Paper. It had been a long while since she really enjoyed the company of a man. She even found herself sometimes getting aroused by the sound of his voice.

The night before, Paper had awoken her by removing the gun from her hand and covering her with a soft blanket. That simple act showed her that he wasn't a bad guy. So she stopped playing possum, and spoke up to request that he give her the gun back and tell her his name. They ended up going down to his room, where they watched television and talked until she fell asleep an hour and a half later.

After she woke up, Leslie was confused with the feelings she had for Paper.

"I want to cook dinner tonight. Do you think we could stop and pick up a few things for me?" Leslie asked.

"We sure can as long as you can cook and it's good!"

"I'm a gourmet cook, nigga. You better ask about me! I'll have you licking your fingers."

"Now if you said it'll have me licking you, I would've asked for dinner right now," he joked.

"Remember you said that after you eat!" she flirted back as they pulled into the parking lot of Pick N Save.

* * *

Trigga, Dream, and Rahji took Tracy for a walk down to the park. It was only a few blocks from his house. The day was warm from the perfect mixture of sun and the cool breeze that came off the lakefront. Rahji rolled around and played in the sand with the dog and a few other kids like no tomorrow.

Dream smiled at the sight of Trigga pushing her as she held onto Tracy on the swing. She thought of the times when Cheez would just stand around and watch her play and not play with her. He never really took the time out to get dirty like the man in front of her. She knew Rahji really liked Trigga, but her newfound affection probably was not good because of the things they were going through. Dream didn't know if Trigga would one day have to vanish or if she would one day have to vanish herself. She shook her head at herself because her thoughts were dangerous. Trigga was not her man. She didn't even know his real name, and here she was having long-term thoughts.

* * *

"Tee-tee, Tee-tee!" Rahji called out while running into the house.

"Hey, you! You look like you had so much fun with all that sand in your hair," Leslie said after giving Dream the why'd-you-let-her-get-sand-in-her-hair look.

"I did. I did. There were a whole lot of friends. I played in the sand with Trigga, Mama, and Tracy!"

As Rahji told her story about the outing, Tracy ran around her feet jumping and barking.

"Okay, baby girl. I got you some new clothes to change into inside your room. So go take a shower and get dressed so you can eat," Leslie told her.

"Baby girl, take your hair down so I can wash it and your Tee-Tee can redo it after dinner," Dream called to her before she ran upstairs, with Tracy right at her heels.

"What you cooking? It smells good already."

"Come help me. You can do the salad and garlic bread."

"What happened for us to get you to cook like this?" Dream asked, looking from her friend over to Paper.

"Whatever! Just get to work!" Leslie said while blushing as she smiled at her friend.

Chapter 13

Want You to Know

After dinner, Leslie and Paper tackled the kitchen. Dream washed her daughter's hair and put her to bed. Afterward, she found Trigga in the game room reading *All Things New* by Nessa Hearts.

"I didn't know you knew how to do that!"

"Do what? I don't know what you're talking about!" Trigga replied.

"Read?" she joked.

"Oh wow! That's how you do me?" he laughed. "I got into reading these urban books years ago when I was in the joint behind them walls."

Trigga shook off the memory of those lost years in prison.

"Hey, I met the writer, Nessa, when I was dancing. She was just getting started with her writing."

Dream took a seat across from him.

"It's kinda exciting to be in the city I only read about."

"How do you like my city so far?"

"It's not as bad as she makes it seem in them books she be writing."

"That's because you ain't been in the hoods yet. Niggas know not to fuck around down here in these parts of the East. Shorewood don't play well with Milwaukee!"

* * *

Paper listened and dried dishes while Leslie told him about herself. She felt so good talking to him. The attraction between them was so strong that it warmed the air.

"After my mother passed, it was up to me to take care of us. My brother got out there in the streets doing his thang. He was selling dope as well as running hoes and shit. And to make a long story short, he ended up in prison for three years for being caught with two ounces of crack," she explained, before she took a sip of her beer.

"Where is he now?" Paper asked, feeling his manhood swell at the sight of her luscious lips around the bottle.

"We fell out!"

"Why, if you don't mind me asking?"

"I found out he was using from one of the girls at the club where I was working. When I brought it up to him, he told me to stay out of his life. I wasn't his mother; he was grown. John was so high that he didn't even look the same. So I told him not to come back around until he was ready to get his shit together. We haven't really talked since."

"That's crazy."

"He called me once on Mom's birthday."

"You ain't tried to help him again?"

"You know I wanted to, but I figured he will come 'round. I'm all he got."

As tears rolled down her cheek, Paper took his hand and wiped them away.

"Shhhh! Don't blame yourself. He's grown! He will come 'round when he's ready. He'll get tired soon," Paper said, sliding his thumb across her lips.

She stopped his hand with hers and kissed it, giving in to what she was feeling. Leslie looked up at him, and he covered her warm soft lips with his. His kiss sent a shock through her whole body. She turned her head, which broke their kiss. She took a deep breath and stepped away from him. She didn't understand what she was feeling. The sexual tension for the opposite sex was foreign to her. She dropped the last glass in the sink and walked out of the kitchen.

* * *

Trigga was awakened in the morning by his cell phone ringing.

"Yeah."

"I know it's early, Trig, but I think you should know that it was that nigga Low Key who sold y'all out," his boy Lucky explained.

"Sold us out how?"

"He set that shit up in Georgia and told Cheez your name, my nigga."

Trigga was now sitting up in bed.

"Where's that nigga Cheez at now?"

"As far as I know, he's in Miami. But I'll find out what I can for you."

Trigga paused in thought.

"Give that nigga my number and make sho' you make him pay you for it."

"Say no mo'!"

The caller hung up just as there was a knock at his bedroom door.

"What up?"

"It's me!"

"It's me, who?" Trigga asked playfully.

"Rahji."

"Oh, okay! Who you looking for, Rahji?"

"You, Trigga," she said, followed by the cutest laugh he had ever heard.

"I'm not here. Come back tomorrow."

"Okay! Mama, Trigga said he's not here, and to come back tomorrow."

Dream laughed.

"Tell him to stop playing and come eat now, and you come on so you can eat this food I cooked."

This was the first real home-cooked breakfast she had cooked in years. She cooked sliced turkey, eggs, grits, pancakes, and homemade biscuits that melted in your mouth when you bit into them.

* * *

After breakfast, Paper and Trigga dressed and hit the streets in chase of the almighty dollar. The two of them cleaned up all the dirty money they made off of pushing dope through the inner-city streets of Milwaukee and a few surrounding counties by investing in gas stations, corner stores, and two apartment buildings. But unlike Trigga, Paper couldn't just walk away from the streets. He was addicted to the fast life and blowing money however he wished.

He pulled up and parked on 37th and Clark, grabbed his Glock .40 out of its stash spot, placed it in his waist, got his black backpack, and got out of his candy-apple green Ford F350. He left his remote Lambo doors open so anyone looking could see the matching interior that was trimmed in rosewood and fiberglass.

"What it do, P. B.? Sam had to make a run right fast to his son's school," the hard-faced thug said as he walked Paper inside the house.

"Yeah. What that lil' nigga do now with his bad ass?"

"I don't know. He's just bad as hell, so there ain't no telling when it comes to Lil Sam."

He then handed Paper a bag.

"Sam told me to give you this and tell you that we short a sticker. Don't ask me how. You gotta talk to him. But he wants you to give us the whole thing. The nigga said he'll put an extra $500 in the next re, and he should want double the next time."

Paper shook his head.

"It's cool, my nigga. I know y'all good for it. But I'ma come get that $500 in like an hour or so."

"Alright, I'll have him call you."

Paper climbed back into his truck and turned up Slim Thug's latest mixtape. The bass from his truck could be heard and felt blocks away as he made his rounds. He made a quick stop to buy the women cell phones and a GPS bracelet for Rahji, just in case.

* * *

Leslie and Dream played school with Rahji to keep her sharp until they could get her enrolled in the local school. School was out in Milwaukee for the summer, so there was no rush. That's if they decided to stay.

Trigga worked on his 1985 Buick Regal, replacing factory parts with custom chrome and gold ones. He worked on his car whenever he was stressed about something. And now sexual tension was thick between Dream and him, which caused him to work overtime on his car. He preferred to keep his relationships with women simple. But something about Dream filled him with a whole new mixture of emotions that he didn't believe he was ready for at this time in his life.

Chapter 14

It's Only a Dream

I paid Lucky two stacks for that nigga Trigga's number, but he didn't have an address on him. Don't fucking nobody know shit too much about the nigga other than that he's in Milwaukee!" Crunch explained.

After writing down the number his man gave him, Cheez turned to the two sexy white girls and said, "If you offer a person enough money, they would give you almost anything. Everybody has a price. You just got to find it."

He then tossed the notepad on the nearby table and pushed the eager girls' heads down so they could finish the oral pleasure they were giving him. He wouldn't use the number until he knew where they were in Milwaukee. He wanted to make Trigga suffer for interfering with his business.

"Big boys play big boy games," he said quietly while lying back on the double-soft pillows.

* * *

At one o'clock in the morning, Trigga was awakened by screams coming from Dream. He had fallen asleep in his comfortable chair while reading, but he immediately rushed up the stairs to her room.

Dream sat up with her back against the cool headboard. She could still see the images of Dice's head exploding. The heat from the house fire made her body sweat. The sound of a branch being blown back and forth outside her window reminded her of the sound made by Scotty's neck when she snapped it. As a kid Dream was taught by her uncle how to fight. He was a great admirer of Bruce Lee and perfected the art of Jeet Kune Do. He taught it to all the children in his family. However, killing Scotty was the first time Dream had to use what she knew to take a life.

Trigga found her sitting up in the bed shaking and crying.

"What's wrong?" he asked sincerely.

She shook her head.

"Nothing! I'm—I'm okay."

She wrapped her arms tightly around her knees. When she looked up at him, he held his hand out to her.

"Come on. Let's go downstairs."

"Is everything good?" Paper asked, suddenly appearing in the doorway behind Trigga with his gun in hand.

"Yeah! She just had a bad dream, bro. She's alright now. I got her."

Paper nodded and then returned to his room.

Trigga helped Dream out of the bed. She was shaking so badly that she had to lean on him for balance as they walked down the steps to the living room, where he had been reading before Dream woke up in a panic. He gently pushed her down into the chair and then went into the kitchen to get coffee. When he returned, Dream was wrapped up in a blanket.

"Did I wake you?"

"No! I was up when I heard you."

He handed her a steaming cup.

"Thanks. You should've left me alone. I'm a big girl. I can handle a little bad dream," she said as she offered him a weak smile.

"I thought you were in pain or something."

He then sat down next to her.

"Look! You're still shaking from it."

"No I'm not. It's just cold in here."

"Okay, if you say so. I don't want to fight. Drink your coffee. It'll help calm you. I put a shot of brandy in it."

Trigga saw that she couldn't keep the cup still as she took a sip.

"Do you want to talk about it?"

"No!"

Dream's answer sounded nervous and unsure, even to her. But after her third sip, her hands were no longer shaking. The brandy-laced drink felt good going down. She balanced the cup on her thigh, and then dropped her head back onto the couch.

"What were you doing down here alone in the dark?"

"I was reading."

Trigga picked the book up from the floor, where it had fallen when he heard her scream. He sat studying her.

"It helps to talk about it. I'm not saying I can get rid of all your monsters, but I can try. Talk to me, Dream. I'll listen."

"Will you?" she asked while looking deep into his eyes.

"I promise not to make fun of you," he chuckled and smiled.

Her hands tightened around her cup.

"I can't let him see me afraid!" Dream said in almost a whisper.

"He who? Cheez?"

"Yes."

Her cup shook again as she answered.

"How were things between y'all, if you don't mind me asking?"

"That muthafucka thinks he's a man, but he's not. He ain't shit! Cheez likes his women weak-minded and sexually talented. His bitch wife is the only one he respects."

"Wait! What were you to him?"

Dream took a deep breath to steady her nerves. She was a bit ashamed, but she knew getting it out was the best way to face it.

"His sex slave."

She trained her eyes on her cup as she spoke.

"I never knew my parents. I grew up in and out of homes. I started dancing when I was fifteen. I got hooked up with an ol' smooth-talking-ass nigga that turned out to be a pimp."

She looked from her cup to study Trigga's expression. The fact that she stripped was the reason she never had a real relationship.

"That's when I met Leslie. She became my rock, saving me from him and showing me I didn't need a nigga for nothing but a good time. I met Cheez when I was nineteen, or more like he met me. He was at the club making it rain on me—and only me—big-balla style. He was there to see me almost every night. Then on one of the club's slow nights, he asked me to skip work and go out to eat with him. I ran it by Leslie first, and she gave me the okay, so I did. Things between us were great, even after he found out I was pregnant, from this bitch named

Star who overheard me talking to Leslie about it. I almost wasn't going to keep my baby girl." Dream shook off the thought. "Now I can't see life without her."

"Don't tell me the nigga flipped the strip on you?" Trigga asked.

"Not the way you're thinking. At least not at first. He was happy about it and made me stop working at the club ASAP. Things were good until he started beating on me. And when I tried to stand up to him is when I became a prisoner. Cheez couldn't break me, and it did something to him."

Dream took a break and sipped her coffee.

"What? Do he think he's untouchable or God himself? He's a bitch for real. One of them fools that had all of what he got handed down to him, and he don't know what it is to get down in the dirt for his. A real bitch-ass nigga." Anger surged through Trigga's blood as he spoke.

Dream stood up, not out of fear of the emotions being expressed by the man next to her, but from the heat building up in her.

"Thank you for everything. I'm going to bed now. Goodnight!"

Trigga didn't know if Dream was leaving because of his rant or what, but he didn't say anything more about it.

"Okay! If you need me, just holler and I'm there," he promised.

Knowing it to be true made her smile.

"Sweet dreams!" she started as she left the room and then stopped at the stairwell. "Thanks again."

"I didn't do nothing but listen."

"Yeah! Well, it was more than that for me. I owe you one."

"I'll remember that, so don't you forget you said it."

Trigga smiled, returned to his seat, and thought about what she had told him about herself. His thoughts easily turned into ones about her beauty. He now wanted her, and he felt that she was what he needed in his life to truly complete it. Because of what he was feeling, Trigga knew he would go to war with hell's angels for her and her child. On that final thought, he lay back on the couch, closed his eyes, and let his thoughts turn into hot and sweaty dreams of them on the very couch where he now slept.

Chapter 15

Never Been Kissed

Hey, Ma!" Rahji announced as she came bouncing through the door.

"Hey, you! What's that you got?"

"Tee-tee and Uncle Paper took me to GameStop and bought me some more games to play, and to Walmart and got me some more toys to play with. Uncle Paper says I had to pick out one book to read, too, because he wants me to grow up to be smart. And then we had ice cream too!" she explained excitedly. "You all wet. What was you doing, Mama?"

"I was working out on the StairMaster. Now I'm on my way to the shower because I'm all sweaty," Dream answered her happy child.

"Okay! I'm going to play my games now. Come play with me when you get out," Rahji said, not waiting for a response as she rushed out of the room.

"Uncle Paper?" Dream repeated her daughter's new name for him while looking over at him and Leslie.

"Yeah? What's wrong with her calling me that? Rahji's my girl."

"Nothing! You spoiling her and making it hard for the next man I get in my life!" Dream told him as she wiped sweat from her face.

"I doubt that very much. But if so, I'm only doing what an uncle do," Paper answered as he handed her one of the bags of things they picked up from the store before walking off to answer his phone.

"Sis, you look like you're in love or something. Is there something I should know about here?"

"Girl, I don't know what I'm doing. But it feels good to be with Paper. He's just so different. He has that thug-type demanding swagger, but he isn't really thuggish. I like it!" Leslie's face flushed as she talked about her feelings. "Girl, what should I do?"

"I say if it feels right, go for it! God has somebody for all of us. So who says you can't get on something different and new?"

"Yeah, something new."

With a pat on the back, Dream left Leslie unpacking the bags in the kitchen as she made her way to go get cleaned up. In her bedroom, she undressed, turned on the shower, and thought of how good it felt to be free of Cheez. She was happy for Leslie and wasn't as scared as she once was, although fear was still there. She stepped under the hot spray of water, closed her eyes, and let the water wash away the dirt and pain of her past. Dream knew she was damaged inside, and she hoped that Trigga was the one who could fix her and give her and her child the life that she dreamed of.

* * *

Later that evening after Rahji and Tracy were put to bed, Dream sat playing games on Facebook. Trigga was out back working on his car for the upcoming car show at Club Brooklyn. Leslie found Paper sitting in the living room watching reruns of NCIS and texting back and forth on his cell phone.

Paper heard someone behind him and turned to see who it was.

"I thought you went to sleep. Is something wrong?"

"Nothing! I'm good. You want some company?"

"Sure," he said as he scooted over so she could sit down next to him. "I didn't know you liked this show," he said after a few long moments of silence.

"I don't even know what it is. I'm watching it because I like you," she answered, not taking her eyes off the television to meet his.

"Oh shit. What's really good?"

"I'm hoping you could show me!" she answered as she looked over at him. "What? I can't try something new?" she asked with a smile.

"Yeah, you can. There's just something different about you."

"I know, but I don't know how to put it into words. It's just something I feel."

"Just say it. I can comprehend pretty well. If I'm off on it, then we can work it out together," he told her, before turning off the 68-inch television and letting the moonlight fill the room.

When Leslie didn't respond, Paper interjected. "Just say it. I'm here for you, Ma."

Leslie let out the breath she was holding on to. "Paper, I've been really thinking about the other day when you kissed me."

"I'm sorry if I offended you. I misread things, and I thought we were past it. I was just really feeling you."

"Was?"

"Yeah! And to be real, I still am."

"Paper, it's good to know that you feel the way I do. I'm really feeling you too. I want to . . . I mean . . ." Leslie began as she tried to prepare herself for his rejection.

"You want to what?"

"Don't make this harder than it is. I haven't been with a man voluntarily ever. The first time I was raped; and after that, I did what I had to do to get by for me and my brother. The truth is you are the first man I've let in like this. Yes, it could be because of all that's going on, but I don't know."

Leslie bit down on her lip the way she did when she was nervous. When Paper didn't say anything and just sat there looking at the floor, she started to get up. "I know it was a bad idea. Forget it."

He grabbed her arm to stop her. "I'm not saying anything because it's new to me to have a woman come at me like this."

Paper then pulled her over to him and covered her lips with his in a kiss. Her body melted into his as she returned it.

"Why's your heart beating so fast?" he asked, before breaking the kiss.

"I'm being such a girl right now," she laughed nervously.

"We don't have to rush nothing. I'll let you lead and I'll follow. I want you to feel good doing this and not hold back. I want all of you to feel good doing this and not hold back. I want all of you. You should know I'm going to give you all of me."

They both began to unbutton each other's shirts. She moaned softly in his ear when his warm hands touched her breasts. The heat between them seemed to change the temperature in the room. Paper pulled her over to him, and she pushed him back with kisses that she dragged down his body. He unbuttoned her pants and helped her as she wiggled out of them. She was lost in the sensation that his hands and fingers were giving her. She then pulled off his pants and let her tongue dance around his belly button. He stopped her just before she could take his hardness in her sexy full lips. He then flipped her and buried his face in her sweet zone, stopping to teasingly kiss her on her inner thighs.

He next fully removed the lacy fabric of what covered her sweet zone with his teeth, no longer wanting to work around them. He took her fingers in his mouth and then guided them between her thighs so she could feel her wetness. He watched her fingers dance around her spot as he stroked himself. She grinded against her palms.

Leslie pulled him over her and placed her wet sticky fingers in his mouth. His hardness made its way inside her warm, wet folds. She dug her nails into his sides as his size stretched her tightness, letting Paper go deeper and deeper. He kissed her forehead, nose, and then one lip at a time. He put passion marks on her neck as her body relaxed.

Leslie now pulled him inside and met his every stroke. They went harder and faster until she felt him begin to swell. She pushed him out of her and took him in her mouth, sucking him until he released.

Chapter 16

A Mother's Love

Cheez answered on the third or fourth ring.

"What you got for me?"

"I got an address for a Patrick Rogers from that punk-ass nigga Low Key before I killed him."

"Who the fuck is he, and what does it got to do with finding that bitch?" Cheez questioned him.

"It's Trigga's closest friend. If we find him, he will take us to Dream."

It had been weeks since Cheez put the word out on Dream, and this was the best information he had received since he was given Trigga's phone number.

"Well, do what you do, killa! I want to know something good soon!"

"I'm already on my way there, fam."

"Alright! Hit me when you know something."

"Say no mo'!" Crunch ended the call.

Hours later, he sat in the home of Rhonda Rogers awaiting her return.

Bully and Ty were the two goons that Crunch had brought with him. They made themselves at home eating her food and watching her DVDs.

Ms. Rogers was a tough, hard-working, and loyal woman who moved to Milwaukee from New York after her husband and oldest son were gunned down in the street by the trigger-happy NYPD as they tried to make a getaway from a drug sweep in the projects. Ms. Rogers was too tired from the double shift she just had worked to notice the sound of her television, which she never left on. As soon as she unlocked her door, it flew open and she was snatched inside by Ty. She tried to scream, but his big hand covered her mouth and suppressed it, and the Glock made her give up the idea altogether.

"Hello, Rhonda!" Crunch said with a smile. "Where is that boy of yours?" he asked as Ty pushed her down in the chair that Bully had put next to them.

"Who are you? I don't know where Pat is!" she told him honestly.

She had never been to the house that Pat shared with Trigga; they always came to visit her. She loved her only living child dearly. But when he chose to follow in his late father's and brother's footsteps, choosing the street life over her, she couldn't take it. That was when she told him not to come home until he did something better with himself. Ms. Rogers never really believed her son when he told her he was no longer on the streets, but she didn't have proof until now. And now she found herself a victim to the cold game of the streets.

"I think you do."

"What did I say? Now get out of my house and leave me alone!"

Crunch nodded his head, and Bully backhanded her in the face so hard that she fell out of the chair. Ty picked her up and Bully hit her again.

"I told you I don't know where he is! Now get the fuck out!" she spat out the bloody words, praying they would have mercy.

But when more blows rained down on her, Ms. Rogers knew there would be none.

"Hold up, damn nigga! Don't you got a mother!" Crunch yelled, which made Bully stop his abuse.

"Yeah, but this bitch ain't her!"

He hit her again before picking up his half-eaten ham and cheese sandwich. It was hard for Ms. Rogers to breathe because her nose was broken. Her eyes were almost swollen shut on her badly battered face. She knew she would die if she didn't tell them something. But if she did, they would kill her child.

Rhonda prayed the Lord's Prayer, welcoming whatever was to be her fate. Her motherly love wouldn't let her give her son to these monsters who would beat on an old woman like a dog. She was fifty-two years old and so very tired. Ms. Rhonda A. Rogers died knowing that she did all she could to protect her son.

* * *

Cheez felt his cell phone vibrating on his hip. He saw that it was Crunch, so he excused himself from Mr. Gomez and made his way to the restroom to return the call. He was hoping it was some good news.

"What it do? I know you got something to put a smile on my face!"

Crunch could hear the irritation in his boss's voice.

"Fo' sho', but Mom wouldn't give up her son even after we beat her for over an hour. The old bitch died for hers."

Cheez couldn't help but respect her for her unselfish deed. It made him wonder if his own mother would do the same for him.

"So why are you calling me when you know I'm in the middle of this shit with Mr. Gomez? You couldn't have saved that shit?"

"Hold up, homie. I got an address where he may be," Crunch said, cutting him off.

"I'm confused. You said his mother didn't talk before she died. So how?"

"She didn't. But we found a letter with his name on it, and the return address on a birthday card and flowers. That's how."

"That's some good shit."

Cheez was pleased with the news, and Crunch knew he would receive a nice bonus.

"I'll be there by noon so we can ride down on them together. I'll be calling you as soon as I touch down."

With that, Cheez ended the call and rejoined the party in a much better mood.

*　*　*

Trigga stormed his Charger recklessly through the streets to get to his best friend's side. He needed to be the first to tell him that his mother had been killed. Trigga felt it was him and his involvement with Dream that got her killed. Things were now very personal between him and Cheez. Not only did he murder his godmother, but he killed Dice, Dice's wife, and two of their three kids. Cheez made it look like a bad house fire to the outside world, but the skillful Milwaukee Fire Department and the CSI team discovered the bullet holes in each of their heads.

Trigga slid the car to a hard stop in front of his house and rushed inside to find his friend and brother crying like a baby in Leslie's lap. Someone had already beaten him to telling him the terrible news.

"I'm sorry, bro! Bro, you hear me? I'm sorry!" His own tears fell from his cold eyes. "Pat! Pat! Paper!" he yelled. "We gonna get them for what they did to Mama, bro! We gonna get them on everything!"

Paper stood and the two hugged each other, both shedding tears for their lost loved one. When the last tear fell, hell would take place on earth for the ones that did it.

"I'ma murder every last one of them muthafuckas involved. On my mama, I'ma get them!" Paper cried out.

A dark cloud hung over the house every second of the day until they laid Paper's mother to rest. Rahji, Leslie, and even Tracy did everything in their power to try to lighten his mood and his heart. Trigga wasn't any better, and Dream had her hands full with him and knowing the truth that this was because of her.

It was surprisingly sunny on the day the James and Rogers families laid Rhonda Rogers to her final resting place. The church was filled with grieving loved ones and friends. Everyone whom her life had touched came to see her home, except for her only son. Paper could not bring up enough strength to go to the church. He needed to remember her the way she was the last time he was with her. Dream went with Trigga to see her away and record it for Paper, just in case he wanted to see how well she was made up after taking such a beating.

Trigga didn't care about the cost. He paid for her to have the best of everything. They had done such a good job with her makeup. In fact, it looked as if she was only sleeping after attending one of her many church services every Sunday. Trigga tossed a handful of dirt onto her casket with a promise to get the ones who took her life.

Chapter 17

Know the Price of Love

Trigga strolled along the beachfront to let the sounds of the Lake Michigan waves crashing ashore briefly take him away from everything. But he was snapped out of his zone by the ringing of his cell phone. He didn't recognize the number, so he knew it had to be the call he had been waiting for. Trigga stopped and answered in mid-step.

"Talk to me, and I'll talk back."

"What up, Trigga my nigga?" the deep voice asked.

"Sleazy Cheezy, is this you? I've been waiting on your call."

Trigga whispered to Dream to call Paper and tell him to be on alert. He thought Cheez might be in the area. He wasn't chancing anything with him anymore, after what had happened to his godmother.

"Ha ha! You's a funny nigga, I see."

"I'll make sure you die laughing. So, why don't you come see me so I can make that happen?"

"Whatever, nigga! But that's what I plan to do. As you see, I can reach out and touch you at any time I get ready. I don't want to cause you no more pain, so why don't you just give me what's mine."

"I have something that belongs to you? Are you sure?" Trigga joked with him.

"Yes, you do. I don't like outsiders in my life. You know how dangerous that could be in our line of work."

He paused.

"No bullshit! I'm willing to pay you for the bitch and cut my losses."

"Yeah. Hoe money is slow money. So let's talk numbers. How much are you willing to pay for the bitch?"

Dream stopped talking on her cell when she heard Trigga and looked over at him, only for him to give her a wink.

"You make the price and set everything up. I'll do it your way. So you know I'm a business man, I pay niggas to handle the street shit."

"What about a half-mil each?"

"So you want $1.5 million, and we go our separate ways? Tell me where and when!" Cheez began.

"No deal! I think I need to ask for more since you answered so quickly."

"Make it $2 million then!"

"It still doesn't make me know you really want her."

"I'll give you that just for the list the bitch took plus another for her and my kid. Take your time and think on it. You got my number. But as you know, my people are on your ass. So please make it easy on yourself. In a sec, you gonna run out of family and friends."

With those final words, Cheez ended the call.

Dream asked Trigga what Cheez said to him. She was still on the line with Leslie and Paper.

"He wants me to sell you to him, but it seems like he wants a list more?"

"I don't have the list. It was with my things I lost in the house fire. So now what?"

"He offered me like $4 million to walk away free."

"Trigga, you're not going to do it, is you?" Dream asked nervously as she looked in his eyes for any sign of betrayal.

"What do I look like? That bitch nigga touched my family, and the only pay I want from him is in blood."

Trigga then turned around and marched back toward the parking lot, with Dream right on his heels.

Once they made it back to the house, he re-capped the whole conversation that he had with Cheez with Paper.

"I think he has my address to my house on 25th and Hadley."

"What makes you think that?" Paper asked while flipping a lighter in his hands.

"It's the only place that Dice or anyone else knows about besides us, and the punk sounded so sure that he could get at us."

"So what we gonna do? You know I'ma murder him on sight for what he did to Moms!" Paper explained while pulling out both of his Glocks and resting them against his head.

The hurt and anger were very clear on his face.

"I wouldn't expect anything less of you. But I gotta think on this shit. We don't know how many of them there are, and we don't want to end up in jail or dead either."

"Now you talking like we don't got shooters on our team. And fuck jail! What the fuck you on, my nigga? That bitch nigga took my mama, and he's going to die for that!"

"Nigga, I'm on what you on. I feel your pain, too. But we got to do it right before we be burying each other, is all I'm saying."

"I don't give a fuck no mo', Trig. He gots to die, and I'm willing to die to make it happen!" Paper explained before he walked off.

"Wait!" Leslie called out, chasing behind him, only to have him slam his car door on her and pull off before she could get into the passenger side.

Trigga knew this was going to be hard because Paper was not in a good state of mind, so he had to come up with something fast. He walked past Leslie on his way to work on his car while leaving Dream sitting in the kitchen. He needed time to think, and he thought hard on it—so much so that he was able to concentrate on the Regal.

He pulled out his 2008 silver and rose Dodge Magnum on 26-inch Asanti rims with rose-colored backgrounds. This was the year before the last Black Sunday car showstopper. He let the bass from Milwaukee's own Baby Drew beat hard out of the two 18-inch subwoofers as he drove toward the inner city. He was in need of some good smoke, so he called his good friend ETO, who was known to have the best kush on the south side of the city. After being told it was good to come through, he turned back up the sounds and got lost in the hard lyrics.

* * *

Dream tossed and turned in bed, restless from all the lustful thoughts that ran through her mind. She was losing the fight with the temptations she faced every day that she spent with Trigga. Dream knew he felt the same way for her as well. She sat up in bed, ran her hand through her hair to put a few loose strands back in place, and then took a deep breath before slipping her feet in her slippers and making her way out of her bedroom.

* * *

Trigga hadn't been home for too long. He sat in his bed watching YouTube videos on his 51-inch smart television, when he heard a soft knock on his bedroom door.

"It's open. What's up?" he called out as he paused the video he was watching.

"Hey, I couldn't sleep and heard your television on when I was making my way to get something to drink," Dream explained.

This was her first time inside his room. She was taken by its feminine style and decor. The room was neat except for his shoes being out of place.

"It was my mother's room. I didn't change it much when I moved in."

"What made you tell me that just now?"

"I don't know. It was the way you were looking around. I felt I should stop the thoughts of another woman being in here. You are the first to ever cross that threshold, except for the female who hung my television, and she was only doing her job," he replied while giving her his sexy smile.

"Yeah right, Trigga. You know you be getting it in here!" she laughed. "You might have one or two in here hiding right now," she joked as she walked in and shut the door behind her.

Trigga noticed the way her nightgown hugged her body when she walked, and the sight made his blood rush. But he wasn't alone. Seeing him lying in bed shirtless in just his boxers made her want to take over her body. She walked straight over to the side of the bed he was on, placed her moist hand on his hard, bare chest, and kissed him. He grabbed her nightgown in a fist, pulling her to him as he matched the passion of her kiss.

Dream unshyly stroked his hardness through his boxers before she slipped her hand inside and released it. He popped the buttons on her gown until it fell to the floor. She climbed onto the bed and pushed him back as she covered his hard chest with kisses before taking him in her mouth. She sucked, slurped, and licked him shamelessly. She paused only to remove his boxers completely, which is when he took over.

Trigga rolled her onto the bed and returned the pleasure, licking and sucking her silk until he got what he was working for. Dream moaned, fought, and pulled her own hair, giving him the first wave of her hot tide. Trigga roughly dragged her to the edge of the bed so he could get in closer.

"Stop! Stop playing with me! I need you in me now!" she demanded in between moans.

She lost her breath when he pushed inside her, slowly rotating his hips, and filling her wetness more and more with each round.

"Oh God. Yes! Please fuck me harder, baby! Make me know you're in this pussy. Yes, baby! Fuck yes!"

Her talking drove him wild, so he pounded in and out of her harder and farther, with her thick legs over his strong shoulders. This gave her sweet pain and wild pleasure. Just as he pulled out of her to show her more of his oral skills, an alarm sounded from his cell phone. He immediately jumped up at the sound.

Chapter 18

I See You

Dream asked Trigga what was going on, knowing it had to be something big to make him stop in the midst of their fuck fest.

"It's the other house. Cheez must be there!"

Trigga grabbed the television remote and pressed a few buttons, until the cameras on the house appeared on his television screen in blocks of four.

Trigga watched as men ran from room to room, before a man Dream called Crunch walked into view on the porch before entering the house. Trigg remembered seeing Crunch before, but not the tall man with long locks pulled back in a tight ponytail. Trigga zoomed in on him.

"That's Cheez's bitch ass! How did you know he would come tonight?" Dream asked, trying to cover herself with a pillow from the bed.

"I didn't. I wasn't 100 percent sure the fool would try me. It's almost two in the morning," he said, looking at the time in the top corner of the screen. "Who he think he is, the police? He must not know the hood don't sleep."

"Are the police going to respond to the alarm, or is it just here?"

"No, because I programmed it not to alert the police. My bro uses the place from time to time to handle shit."

"So what now? You just gonna let him get away?"

"For tonight, yeah. I know he's here and on the right trail. Now I can deal with him on my terms when the time is right."

Trigga hit the button on the remote and shut off the television. He then hit another button that filled the room with the soulful voice of Marsha Ambrosius.

"But right now, we need to finish what we started!"

* * *

"There ain't nobody here! We looked all through this bitch," one of Crunch's men, Mike, reported when his boss walked inside the house.

"What the fuck!" Cheez snapped. "Where are these muthafuckers at? Find something with some information on it. Something I can use to lead me to them now."

The men began to tear apart the house at Cheez's command.

"This is the right place. Here's the nigga right here!" Crunch said as he handed his boss a picture off of the living room wall. The photo showed Trigga and his sister on a prison visit the weekend before she was killed.

"I want you to find this bitch in this picture. Find me something to make this muthafucker come out from wherever he hiding!" Cheez ordered, before returning to his rental car.

No one knew they were being watched by tiny cameras hidden in the motion sensors throughout the house. Once Crunch returned to the car, Cheez told him to have someone stay behind and watch the house in case they returned to it. He then told him to take him back to the hotel.

Chapter19

Please Don't

P aper woke up from a nightmare about his mother being beat to death. In it, no matter how fast he ran, he couldn't get close enough to save her. His body was drenched with sweat. He got up and went to the bathroom. His hands were still shaking from the dream as he splashed cold water on his face. It did nothing to help him regain his composure. Paper closed his eyes as he took a few deep, slow breaths to steady himself. When he reopened them to look in the mirror, he saw Leslie standing behind him in the doorway.

"Did I wake you?"

"No, not really. I couldn't sleep. I'm worried about you."

She walked in and wrapped her arms around him from the back.

Paper turned to face her. "I had that dream about my mother again," he said.

"I know. You kept calling her name and tossing and turning." She laid her hands on his chest. "You hit me a few times too."

"I did? I'm sorry, I didn't mean to." He kissed the top of her head as he hugged her. "I finally got someone worth taking to meet her and she's—she's!"

"Stop it, bae! I know you didn't mean to. It's okay," Leslie said as she led him back to bed. "It's gonna be okay. I know it's hard now, but the pain won't last. It won't be this great forever. Bae, I'm here for you to cry on and with as long as you need me to be."

Paper looked into her eyes and saw nothing but truth.

"Thank you," he said, before he kissed her soft lips.

"You don't have to thank me," she told him as she laid her head on his chest and curled her body around his.

Paper's pain wouldn't let sleep take him again. What he found in dreamland was too suffocating to deal with.

"I got to do something now! I can't sit around and wait. It was *my* mother he killed, not theirs," he thought.

When he heard Leslie's light snore, he slid from under his sleeping beauty.

"That punk took mine from me, so I'ma take all of his from him before I take his life."

His mind was racing a mile a minute as he dressed. He then grabbed both guns and his keys as he tip-toed out of his bedroom. At this point the only thing on his mind was murder, and the only thing in his heart was pain.

* * *

Dream awoke in the morning surprised to find herself really in bed with Trigga. The night before was almost unreal to her. He touched her as if she was made just for him. She ran her hand down his body to find him hard and ready for another round. The feel of his warm hardness in her hand made her wetter than she was from her memories of the night before. Feeling bold, she covered his hardness with sweet wet kisses before taking it in her mouth.

The sensation that Trigga felt from her warm wet mouth woke him up.

"Good morning to you too."

Dream stopped just long enough to greet him, before she went back to work on him.

"Oh shit! If I would've known this was how you like to wake a nigga up, I would've taken you down a long time ago."

"Is that right?" she asked, straddling him, easily sliding all the way down his hardness while slowly taking it all in.

She twirled her hips, showing her skill as a dancer by bouncing up and down on him at the same time. Trigga grabbed her butt and met her with matching force. Every time he brought her down, she came harder and wilder. After she felt him release his essence inside her, she collapsed on his chest and covered his lips with kisses. She then rolled off of him and walked into the bathroom.

"Can you turn on the shower for me, sexy?"

"Only if I can get in with you," she called back.

They both took their time washing and exploring each other under the hot spray of water. Trigga stepped out first, but not before making her cum uncontrollably for the second time that morning.

* * *

Leslie awoke to an empty bed. She got up and went to the bathroom, got herself together, and walked down to the kitchen to wake everybody with the smell of a home-cooked breakfast. Trigga was the first to show.

"Good morning, Mrs. Butterworth's."

"You got jokes this morning, I see."

"Yeah, and I'm just getting warmed up."

They laughed and continued to small talk until Dream walked into the kitchen looking confused. They both noticed as she walked out of the kitchen and then back in again.

"Hey, girl, I see somebody's looking brand new!" Leslie teased.

"Whatever! Ain't nobody say shit to you about your late-night creeps!" Dream countered her comment.

"Didn't think I knew about that, did you?" she teased as she gave Leslie a wide smile.

"What am I missing here?" Trigga asked, not following their conversation.

"Oh, don't act like your boy ain't told you about him and her. We know how y'all niggas talk when you get some good-good."

"Oh shit, I thought you didn't do niggas, but I see you just had to get one of us Milltown niggas in your life."

They all shared a good laugh.

"Where's that nigga at now? Is he still asleep?" Trigga asked.

"Where's baby girl at? I didn't see her in her room, and Tracy's down here on her own bed asleep."

"I don't know where Paper went, and Miss Rahji might be in my bed since you wasn't in yours last night," Leslie answered as she made pancakes.

"Nope! She's not there. I just came out of there," Dream told her.

Trigga went to get the newspaper off the porch.

"I wonder where Paper ran off to this early?" Trigga stated when he walked back into the kitchen.

"I don't know. He didn't say. Maybe he went to the store to get some more juice and blunts, since somebody used the last of everything last night," Leslie said while looking at Trigga, who was the last person to come back to the house last night.

"Call him and see if he took my baby with him."

"Okay! Oh shit!" Trigga said out loud.

"What?" the women asked at the same time.

"How was he last night?"

"He was upset from his nightmare, but he was good after we talked about it. We went right to sleep after. Well, I did anyway. He was up and gone by the time I woke up."

"He's not answering his phone. It's going straight to voice mail now, or he's sending me there," Dream told them, with worry shading her face.

"I think he's got Rahji with him," Trigga spoke up while dialing Paper's number himself from his cell.

"Oh God! No! What is he going to do with my baby?" Dream wondered as she broke down crying.

"Hey! Could he see in the other house like you could last night?"

"Yeah, but he would have said something to me."

"You didn't say shit to him when you seen it, so you can't say that."

"What y'all talking about?" Leslie asked while turning off the stove.

"Cheez is here. They kicked in the door to my house on 25th last night."

Trigga then filled in Leslie on what they had seen last night.

"Dream, I know he won't hurt her, trust me."

"How can you say that, Trigga? What made you say that?" Dream asked almost in a panic now.

"I didn't mean nothing. I just don't want you worrying. I'll find them. Y'all stay here in case he comes back."

"Fuck that! I'm going to come with you, Trigga. If Paper did something to my baby, I'ma kill him!"

"Dream. Dream! Let's not think like that. He's not a monster. I'll stay here and keep trying his phone. He might not be able to hear it for some reason," Leslie said to Dream as she and Trigga walked out to his car.

Leslie went right to dialing Paper's number as soon as they pulled away. She was praying each time that he would pick up. She thought about something he told her he liked to do. So she called Dream.

"Hello! Do you got her?" she answered on the first ring.

"No, I just called to tell y'all to check the lakefront because he told Rahji he would let her see the sunrise one day."

"Okay! We're on our way there first. Trigga told me that he liked to go there in the morning sometimes."

"Call me as soon as you hear something!"

"I'll do the same!" Dream promised, before ending the call and then praying for her child's safe return.

Leslie went back to Paper's bedroom to check if he forgot his phone at home, since he wasn't answering. She couldn't let herself believe the man she was falling for would do something harmful to a child.

"Bae, please answer!" she said while dialing his number once she found the cell phone wasn't in the room.

Chapter 20

What Am I Doing?

Paper drove through the streets surrounding his mother's home, but he couldn't bring himself to ride down the block, let alone go inside the house in which she was killed. Tears burned his eyes as he thought about all the times she chased him down these same blocks that he now circled. His tears fell as he thought about punishing sleeping beauty in his back seat for the sins of her father.

He remembered watching Rahji run and play with Tracy the first day he had met her. He remembered how good it felt to see her smiling face and hear the child's sweet laughter. He also remembered how good her little hugs felt and how she gave them away so freely.

All of this filled his mind, and he knew he couldn't go through with it. It was senseless to take her life. It wouldn't bring his mother back or give him the peace he needed. He wanted her father and the flunky who pulled the trigger, not this child. He was not this type of monster—the kind he needed to be to burn a child.

"Hey! Good morning, Uncle Paper!" Rahji sang, breaking him from his thoughts with her sleepy little voice.

"Good morning, princess. Do you know what you want to eat this morning yet?" he asked her, swallowing hard to ease the tightness in his throat.

"I don't know, Uncle Paper. Hey! Why are you crying? Do you still miss your mama?" she asked, after noticing his tears.

"Yeah, I do miss her. I miss her very much, sweetheart. But something flew in my eyes. That's why I'm crying," he lied, not wanting Rahji to worry about him.

"Mama said she's with God now; and when people we love die, God makes them our angels to keep us safe, so they are always with us."

She hugged his neck once Paper stopped at a red light.

"I'll remember that. Thank you! Now you can have anything you want. So tell me what you got a taste for, and I'll make it happen for you."

With that, Paper knew he would be taking the child back home to her mother and letting his brother do what he did, so they could spill his mother's murderer's blood on her grave. Paper didn't know how he would explain his actions to everybody, but he picked up his cell to return all the calls he missed. He was hoping the right words would come out of his mouth when they answered.

* * *

The candy-painted Charger skillfully raced up the streets toward Ms. Rogers's house after circling the lakefront and its surrounding parks.

"I'ma kill him if he hurts your baby! But I know he's not going to. Bro ain't like that. He ain't that kind of person. We're really blowing this up to be more than it is."

Trigga prayed this to be true as he tried to convince Dream.

"How can you be so sure when he took her and didn't tell me and won't answer his phone? Did you think he was the kind of nigga that would do that?"

"Dream, you're right in your thinking as a mother, but I know him better. In my heart, I know he wouldn't. I shouldn't have jumped the gun in the first place."

Trigga shook his head at the driver in front of him, who almost made him run into the back of his car while trying to catch the young women on the bus stop.

"You got to trust me right now. He's going to get up with us soon. I promise he will!" Trigga said, trying to calm her down.

The car made a turn up Lisbon onto Walnut when Trigga heard the all familiar "Yo Gotti" ringtone he had programmed for Paper.

"What's on your mind, bro? Where you at?"

"Where my baby at? Let me talk to her!"

Paper heard Dream in the background and felt bad about making her worry.

"What up, bro? Why y'all tripping? The princess is good. She's with Uncle Paper. Tell mama bear to calm down. I took her to see the sunrise before I tried going by my mom's house. We didn't make it. I couldn't bring myself to take that step, bro."

"Okay! Where y'all at now?"

Trigga thanked God he was right about Paper, but he could sense an undertone in his voice that they would address between one another.

"We on our way back to the house. We 'bout ten blocks away."

"Alright! I'll see you when we get back. I'm up here by Mom's house right now," he explained while making a U-turn. "Bro, I first got to stop and drop off some cash to Moe at Eastside Auto, and then I'll be there. But put Rahji on the phone so she can talk to her mother. You had her all worried and shit!"

"Okay! Princess, your mother's on the phone for you," Paper told her as he handed Rahji the cell.

"Hello?"

"Hello! Dream, I didn't mean to scare you. Sorry about that," Paper apologized.

"It's okay. It's just all this shit going on. And with Cheez showing up here last night, I kinda went there. So I'm sorry too!"

"Hold up! What you mean Cheez showed up last night? He showed up where?"

"Oh, you didn't know! Here, Paper, I'll let your brother tell you about it." She knew she had said too much.

"No! Here's Rahji, but don't hang up. I want to talk to Trigga about what you said."

He passed the phone over to Rahji so mother and child could talk. When Rahji was done explaining to her mother how pretty the sun looks coming out of the water and about her not knowing what she wanted for breakfast, she passed the phone back.

"Now put that seatbelt back on right."

"Okay, I did already," Rahji said, holding her arms up to show off her seatbelt for his approval.

"Hello, Dream?" Paper asked, turning his attention back to the call.

"It's me, bro. I heard you, and I'll tell you about that shit when we make it back to the house. You know how I feel about this phone shit!" Trigga reminded him.

"But how do you know that he's here? Never mind! I'll see you when you get here. I'm pulling up to the house now."

Trigga agreed and then ended the call. Paper put pressure on the gas and sped up his truck. He knew he messed up by taking Rahji the way he had, but his emotions were all over the place. He felt his blood pressure rise when he heard the person who took his mother from him was in town. Paper couldn't wait to find out everything Trigga had to tell him.

When they pulled in, Leslie was sitting on the back porch smoking a Newport.

"Hey, Tee-tee!" the child greeted with a hug once she sprang from the truck.

She then saw Tracy at the screen door eagerly waiting for her as she ran inside to play with the dog.

"What up? You alright?" Leslie asked flatly.

"Yeah, I just talked to bro a few minutes ago. They'll be here in a few." He stood in front of her holding her eyes with his own. "Les, I'm sorry for scaring y'all like that. I should have said something to you. I just! We went to the lake and to Mom's house. Well, I tried to go but couldn't do it." He moved in to hug her, but she wasn't moving.

"So why didn't you answer your damn phone for me, Paper?"

Leslie then stepped out of reach and stopped him with her hand. She didn't want him in her space.

"I said I'm sorry, Les! But I didn't hear it. It's still on silent mode from last night when that stupid ass kept calling!" he explained, referring to an ex turned stalker.

"Look, Paper! If we are going to be something, you can't be doing shit like this to me. I don't just give my heart to any nigga."

She then gave in and hugged him tightly.

"And let me holla at ol' girl to tell her what's up, because I don't share."

"Okay, ma. You got that. But what if she don't want to go? Can we?"

"Boy, don't play!" she cut him off. "I don't do sloppy seconds. If we add someone to this, she's going to be new to the both of us. And I'ma pick her, so we won't have none of this childishness."

Once Paper agreed, she rewarded him with a kiss. They then went into the house where Leslie made him and Rahji the breakfast they had missed out on.

Chapter 21

This How You Play

Cheez sat poolside with his lovely wife, Amilia, half-watching their kids playing in the cool water with a few friends and family.

"Baby, what's on your mind? You look stressed!" Amilia said as she rubbed sunscreen on one of the children who was looking a little too red for her liking.

"Do I? I'm sorry, love. There's just a lot going on right now, and my guys aren't making any progress to fix it!" he explained, eyeing his cell phone that was setting on the deck table.

Amilia noticed and snatched it out of his reach.

"No! You promised me you wouldn't bring that street shit into our home. This weekend is supposed to be for me and the kids," she pouted.

"What are you talking about? I don't have anything in our home, and I'm here!"

He sat up in his seat.

"Baby, if it's on your mind to the point that it has you all spaced out when you're with us, to me that's the same thing. I'm not playing second today."

"Okay! I see what you mean, ma. I'm sorry!"

Cheez turned in his seat taking in Amilia's very curvy body. She was dressed in a two-piece Dolce & Gabbana swimsuit that made his blood rush.

"Is there something I can do to make it up to you?"

"Since you asked, yes! There is something you can do."

"What is it? Anything to make my queen happy."

He gave her a small sexy smile.

"Let me have my husband for the next few days with no interruption. That means, you let what's-his-face do his job and handle all that street stuff while I handle you."

It had been weeks since he touched or even slept in the same room with Amilia. Cheez knew what she wanted.

"Okay, done! But only if you let me take you out of that swimsuit right now."

He reached up and ran his finger along her top while lightly touching her breast and causing her nipples to spring to life.

"Papi, what about the kids?"

"What about them? They're okay. Look at them having a good ol' time. I'll make it quick."

"No you won't, papi! You owe me, and I want all that I got coming."

"You know I like it when you talk to me like that. Go ahead, and I'll meet you in the bedroom in a second. I'm just going to let Crunch know you got me on punishment for the next few days, and tell the men to be on point with the kids since we're going to be in the house for awhile."

"Okay! Don't make me wait too long. It's been long enough already."

"Amilia, can I watch you play with whatever toy you use to get off with when I'm away on my trips?"

"Papi, why do you want to see all of a sudden? What are they telling you?"

"It's not like that, beautiful. I just want to know what I'm up against."

"Okay! I got just the one for you to enjoy with me."

She smiled enticingly after kissing him on the corner of his mouth and handing him back his phone.

Cheez watched her full hips sway as she walked into the house to prepare what she had in store for him. When he was sure she was out of earshot, he called Crunch, who was still in Milwaukee. Cheez told him that he had to handle everything on his own because Amilia was tripping about him not spending enough time at home. Cheez didn't have to explain to Crunch the importance of keeping his wife happy, since everyone knew that Cheez was married into the cartel.

After the call with Crunch, Cheez put his security team on point. He then freed his locks from the hair tie and let them fall loosely over his shoulders as he made his way up the stairs to his wife. He found her and a very attractive Latina in the marble hot tub. The sexy girl sat straddling his wife as they kissed passionately. Cheez was shocked and turned on at the same time.

"My, my! What's going on here?"

Amilia saw his erection in his shorts and knew he wasn't upset with her.

"We're just getting warmed up for you, baby!"

She tapped the girl's butt, and the woman stood up like a well-trained pet to let Cheez get a good look at her voluptuous nude body. Her body was covered with a big colorful dragon tattoo and flowers on her right side.

"So, is this what you've been doing when I'm away?" Cheez asked, closing the door behind him.

"Yeah, part of it. I had to send the other one away because her monthly friend wouldn't let her play the way I need her to for you," Amilia answered, pushing the girl down on the rim of the tub.

Cheez didn't know his wife was into women, and he couldn't believe he was watching her fingering and fondling the breasts of another woman while she stared into his eyes.

"Are you just going to watch me or help me play with this sweet pussy?" she asked while sticking her cum-covered fingers in her mouth.

Cheez kicked off his sandals before climbing inside the tub, where he quickly replaced Amilia's fingers with his lips to taste the girl on her mouth.

"Do you like the way she tastes?"

"You make anything taste good, ma. But I'll tell you just how much I like it in a second."

He dropped down between the girl's short legs and then ran his tongue up her inner thigh until he reached her clean-shaven mound. He skillfully buried his face inside and worked her love button with his tongue and fingers.

Watching her husband do this to the young woman drove Amilia wild. She grabbed a handful of the girl's long curls and kissed her while she touched herself. The sounds the girl made from the pleasure that Cheez was giving her made Amilia a bit jealous.

"Papi, I need you too!" she begged, turning around and bending over for him to enter her tightness from the back.

Cheez stood up and happily blessed his wife with long powerful thrusts. The girl wrapped her legs around Amilia's shoulders so she could get her where she needed her to be. Soon, Amilia brought her to uncontrolled

130

eruptions with her knowing tongue. Amilia came right behind her lover as Cheez was pushed out of his wife by the girl who hungrily covered his hardness with her mouth. Amilia quickly recovered and joined her as they licked and sucked him until he busted. The women fought to catch his cum. Amilia then pushed the girl out of the way and sucked her husband hard again.

"I want to see you fuck the shit out of my bitch!"

"Oh yes, papi. Fuck me! I want you to fuck me hard!" she begged.

Cheez then pushed her back onto the floor that surrounding the tub, pinned her legs down, and gave her what she asked for. Then the threesome carried on until the sun was replaced with stars.

Chapter 22

Shoot Your Shot

Rahji was in the tub with her best friend, Tracy, who was trying hard to jump in with her. The sight of it brought a smile to Dream's lips. But on the inside, she was struggling with the plan that Trigga and Paper had come up with to use her and her child as bait to get back at Cheez.

"Any problems in there you need mama to help you with?" Dream asked from her place in the doorway.

"Nooo! I mean yeah. Can you wash my back, please! I'm still too little to reach it."

Dream happily washed her baby girl's back the way she used to when Rahji was smaller. They laughed and played as they splashed water back and forth at each other.

When Rahji was all clean, she stepped out of the tub and Dream draped a dry towel around her. Rahji then ran from the bathroom to her bedroom, leaving wet footprints behind. This reminded her mother of the "Footprints" poem that she used to read to her daughter when she was in Sunday school.

"Rahji, after you get dressed for bed, you can go down and watch the movie with Tee-tee and Paper. But as soon as it's over, I want you in bed, okay?"

"Okay, Mama!"

Rahji rushed to get dressed as Dream cleaned up the bathroom and drained the tub. A few short minutes later, Dream heard her calling from her room.

"Did you call me, baby girl?" Dream asked while walking over to Rahji's bedroom doorway.

"Yeah!"

"Here I am. What's up?"

"Can Tracy sleep in here with me, please?"

"You know what? I'ma let you have that. Yes, she can! But I don't want to hear it when you don't want her in the bed with you and she won't leave."

"She loves me, and I love her, so I ain't gonna ever not want her in bed with me," Rahji said, giving her mom a hug and kiss before rushing down to watch the movie.

* * *

After carrying the sleeping princess up to her room, Leslie returned to find Paper on his cell phone. She took it from his hands and powered it off. She did the same with the other phone, and then placed both of them on the nightstand and began unbuttoning his shirt.

"Why did you just do that?" he asked, not putting up a fight.

"It's time for bed, and I'm ready to lie down without all this in my ear," she explained as she finished up with his shirt. "I'm sure you can take care of the rest. I'm going to get a water. Do you want one?"

"Yes! With ice, please?" he told her as he quickly finished getting undressed and back in bed.

Leslie returned a few moments later with the drinks, and she then climbed into the bed beside him, cuddling close.

"This is nice."

"Les! Talk to me. I can tell something is on your mind."

"I'm just thinking about the plan to use them for a trap to get Cheez's crazy ass."

"What concerns you about it?"

"Well, what if he don't come himself and he sends that fool Crunch to do the deal for him?"

"That's a chance we got to take. But I'm sure Trigga will let him know that if there's no him, then there's no deal. Dream knows the nigga best, and she's the one who said he will want to come in person to get his hands on her."

"But what if—?"

"Les, stop it! Don't worry yourself sick with what-ifs. Let's get some sleep right now, and we can all talk more in the morning. Trigga is the best at what he do. Trust me."

"Okay," she agreed as she moved in closer to him.

"Give me a kiss goodnight."

She tilted her head to meet his lips.

Leslie wrapped herself around him the way he had gotten used to her sleeping. Even though Paper had just told Leslie not to worry, he could not help but think of the what-ifs to the scenario Trigga had planned. But when Paper felt Leslie's warm tongue on his nipple and her soft hand slip into his boxers, he forgot all else on his mind.

* * *

Not one of Crunch's men was able to come up with any more information on Paper and Trigga. He was getting restless and sick of chasing down Dream for Cheez. Crunch felt he deserved to enjoy himself and live it up just as he imagined his boss was doing back at home. Crunch decided that he and his men would take a break from surveilling Trigga's and Paper's two homes—the ones they knew about anyway. He took three of his five men out to enjoy Milwaukee's night life. The two men he left behind had plans with two cleaning ladies from the superb motel at which they were holed up.

Crunch thought it would be best to hit Textures Nightclub as a show of appreciation for his men. They went to the House of Fades to get fresh haircuts and shaves, and then to Playmakers for new outfits. These were all the places they kept hearing about on the radio, and they found the experience was well worth the money they spent.

* * *

The line was out the door when they pulled up to the club.

"Fam, ol' Milltown got some bad bitches."

"I see! I see! You must be talking about shorty in that short-ass dress over there?" one of Crunch's men said as he pointed toward the middle of the line.

"Shit! Y'all fools trying to look at one and missing all this here!" Crunch commented as he let down the window of the rented Jeep Commander to get at one of the beauties crossing in front of him.

"Nooo! If you want to talk to me you going to have to get up out of that truck. I don't walk up on cars I don't know," the sexy dark beauty schooled him while waiting for Crunch to make his move.

"Hold up! Hold up! Give a nigga a chance to get out of this muthafucka."

Crunch then jumped from the SUV and was followed by Mike and Bully. Ty found a parking spot not far from the entrance of the club. Once Crunch had all his men by his side, he freely gave $400 to the big bouncer at the door to let them and the three women skip the line. For this, they were seated in VIP with their first rounds of drinks on the bouncer.

Chapter 23

Get the Party Started

After going over the plan Trigga had come up with, for the tenth time that day, Leslie placed a call to Cheez, just as she was instructed. After the third try, a female with a heavy Spanish accent answered.

"Hello?"

"Umm, is Cheez around?"

"Yes, but who are you?" Amilia questioned Leslie.

"That don't matter. Just tell him I can show him dream works. He is a smart man, so he should know what I'm talking about."

Amilia walked into their game room and found Cheez lying across a chair watching the kids playing Xbox on the big-screen television.

"Baby! Here, you better take this."

She handed him his cell.

"The bitch didn't give me her name. She only said that she can show you your dream works or something like that."

He accepted the phone, stood up, and walked into his office.

"Who is this?"

The sound of his voice made Paper's blood burn, but he held it together. He knew if all went well, he would have his revenge for what was taken from him.

"I know you know me well enough to know I love money. So I'm hoping we can do some business. You get what you're looking for, and I get what I love."

"And you think you have something I want? Look, I'm a man of many businesses, so you got to be more specific, miss, or I'm going to hang up. I don't have time to waste."

"You know this Leslie, Cheez! Don't play with me. I know you know my voice."

"I really didn't catch until but now. Where are you and my bitch?"

"Let's talk money before we talk that."

The line went silent for more than thirty seconds before he spoke up again.

"Why should I trust you? The last I checked, you and the bitch were like sisters."

"Look, Cheez, I'ma simple-life bitch. I ain't about being shot at and constantly running for my life because a bitch is having a sissy fit. I didn't know it was going to be all this shit here, and I'm not with this. I just want my life back," Leslie explained with such passion that everyone in the room thought she was telling the truth.

"So you're telling me you will sell out your best friend? What's your price?"

"Yes! But you got to promise not to kill her or kill me."

"I can do that. What's your price?"

"Well, I know you offered Trigga like a million dollars, but I know you better. I know you were just going to kill him and take them from him."

The line went silent again.

"That might've been true, but he's not you. So how much do you want?"

141

"Look, I just lost every fucking thing fucking with Dream and this shit. I know she's never going to talk to me after this, so I need enough to start over here in Wisconsin, get me by until I get back on my feet."

"I understand, but you're not telling me a price."

"I don't know! Just throw one at me you think is fair."

"Alright! If you're serious, I'll give you $150K. But if you're trying to play me, I will kill you myself."

"Man, Cheez! You don't got to be threatening me."

"I was just letting you know."

"Oh, believe me, I know. I'm barely living now because of you."

"Okay then. Let's see how we can do this, so you'll feel safe. It's clear that we have trust issues."

They could hear the excitement in Cheez's voice as he spoke. It was getting harder for Paper to control his anger, so he motioned for her to wrap up the call.

"How about you figure that out and get back to me with it. I got to go before she comes looking for me."

Leslie ended the call, tossed the phone onto the table, and then wiped her sweaty hands on the back of her cutoff jeans.

"How was that?"

"I think the bitch is going for it, for real. I could hear it in his slimy voice."

Dream stood up looking at the floor half-hugging herself as she answered.

"Good! That's what we want!" Paper said, checking his building rage.

"Hey! Y'all relax!" Trigga told the women, upon seeing how nervous they were. "We got this. It'll all be over soon."

* * *

Cheez set down his cell on his desk and then turned around to find Amilia standing behind him with two cold beers in her hands. She took a swallow from one as she handed the other one to her dumbfounded husband.

"Sit down and let's talk about that bitch, Dream, and our daughter, Rahji," she said, letting him know she knew more than what she could have heard from the call.

"How do you know about them?" he asked, taking a seat on the corner of the desk.

"Love, I'm a Gomez by blood. There's not too much I don't know about mines," she replied as she stared directly into his eyes.

Cheez dropped his head in thought for a quick second.

"Amilia, I'm—!"

"There's no need for that. You're my husband, and I'm not going to let no little stripper bitch take you from me."

"I promise that would never happen!"

"Good! So let's talk about how we plan on getting our daughter back from that whore."

Amilia then walked over to Cheez, stopped between his legs, and kissed him.

"I want you to kill that bitch with your own two hands. And know that this is the last time you have an outside baby on me!" she spoke up.

Hearing her say those words to him excited him. Cheez pushed by her, locked the door so their kids wouldn't walk in, and then turned and slapped her butt two quick times. Amilia smiled and held her face as she watched him unbuckle his pants. Cheez grabbed her by the arm, roughly spun her around, bent her over the desk, and entered Amilia from behind. She loved every inch of the fucking that Cheez was giving to her. She proved it to him by throwing it right back at him.

Chapter 24

Ingredients

ETO emerged from the rear of his most profitable weed spots on 7th and Madison on the lower south side of the city. One of his lookouts informed him that Trigga's car just rounded the one-way. A moment later, the wet shine of the candy-painted Dodge Magnum showed them their clear reflection when it stopped in front of them.

"I see you on point, my nigga!" Trigga greeted him when he got out of it.

"Always. But when you going to sell me this bitch here, Trig?"

"Soon, homie. I ain't done playing with it just yet!"

He waved and the passenger let down her window.

"What's up?" Dream asked, feeling the hot summer air on her face.

"E, this is Dream, who I was telling you about."

"What it do? He didn't tell me how fine you is!" ETO flirted.

"No? Well, what did he tell you?" she asked while looking in the direction that he had waved his hand.

"Trig told me you like to smoke and that you're from Miami."

"Oh did he?" she answered as she looked Trigga's way with a smirk on her lips. "I don't smoke like that, but it's nothing but the best when I do."

Soon a short, enthusiastic teenager strolled up speaking to ETO in Spanish as he handed him a jar of weed that resembled fruit blossoms.

"I bet they don't got this shit here back home. If they do, then somebody down there owes me!" ETO said, passing the jar over to Dream.

"I'll be sure to let you know later. Right now I'm going to let y'all talk, and stop letting this hot air in."

When she closed the window, the men walked up the block at a slow pace. It was clear that Trigga was running down his plan to ETO and asking for his help.

"I got a chick that works at the motel where I think them fools are staying. She was telling me about a muthafucka running some wannabe gangster shit to her. I'll hit her up on it."

Trigga slowed down the pace even more while hanging on ETO's every word. Trigga knew he came to the right man for assistance. ETO was a hood boss that still loved to bust his guns anytime he got the chance. It was his way of showing his team that he would die and kill for them, and he expected nothing less from them in return.

From the next block over came the sound of gunshots followed by what sounded like a car crash. This was Trigga's cue to move around.

"Say, my nigga, we on for that as you can see. I got to handle this lil' shit right now."

ETO didn't wait for Trigga's response. Instead, he rushed off and disappeared through the nearest gangway behind a few of his men.

* * *

Over on the north side of the city, Paper rode down on his old friend Sam and his team of goons right in the middle of a shootout of their very own. As soon as Paper stepped from his truck, a juvenile girl and a boy ran up on him fully strapped with water guns and buckets of balloons.

"We going to ask you one time!" the boy said while taking aim.

"Paper! Who you with, us or them?" the girl questioned, already drenched from the water fight.

Sam had already warned him of the water war going on, so Paper had come prepared for the scene.

"Y'all should know not to run up on a boss. Get 'em!"

With that, Leslie and Rahji sprang up from the bed of the truck spraying the two with the almighty Super Soaker.

"I ride with my niggas!" Paper told then, reaching in and grabbing a water gun from the floor of the truck.

He, Leslie, and Rahji sprayed their way from the truck to the house.

"Wow! I ain't had this much fun in a long time!" Leslie said while drying her face.

"Me neither!" Rahji agreed excitedly. "I need some more water, Tee-tee!"

Lil Sam ran into the house completely drenched from the ongoing water war.

"Man, they on one! They got a water hose."

He scanned Rahji from head to toe.

"Hey, little ma. What's your name?"

His dad, Paper, and E-Bay laughed at the youngster.

"Man, get somewhere with your bad ass!" E-Bay teased him.

"Hey, nigga. Don't be a hater all your life!" Lil Sam told him.

"Bro, these two lovely ladies are Leslie and Rahji!" Paper introduced. "And this is Sam and his son, Lil Sam. And the guy who just ran out the door is E-Bay."

"Hey, thanks for coming through for a nigga. Y'all right on time. I owe you one," Sam said as he set down his water gun.

"I'm glad you said that, because that's kinda what I came to talk to you about."

"Well, I'll let you two talk. We'll all go outside, and I'll keep an eye on Rahji and little Romeo."

Leslie excused herself, grabbed her Super Soaker, and then followed the kids out of the house.

Paper ran down the situation and the plan to Sam. Once he was done, Sam said, "As you can see, we don't duck no action over these ways. I'll make sure lil' mama's good. We can use the daycare to get this here done. I got you, my nigga. You ain't never let me down in my time of need, so it's only right a nigga be here for you in yours."

After making a few adjustments to Sam's part in the plan, they ran outside to rejoin the fun of the water fight turned block party.

* * *

Crunch didn't get Cheez's text until the next afternoon when he rolled off the beauty that he had picked up at the club, for the second time since they woke up. When he did pick up his phone, the last text informed him that Cheez would be there in less than two-and-a-half hours. Crunch rushed the girl up, gave her some cash, and promised to get up with her as soon as he could. Then he called to get his men on point so the boss wouldn't have anything to say about them not doing their jobs.

Chapter 25

Nervous

Cheez stared at his wife, who was reading the latest issue of *Better Homes & Gardens*, and he thought about the conversation he had with Leslie. She agreed to his price, but he had to give her half up front to show that he wouldn't try to renege on their deal; and if he did, she would have something for her troubles. He brought Amilia along to kill her curiosity about Dream. For the first time, he wondered if his wife would really watch him kill her. The truth was that he didn't know if he was really ready to be rid of Dream just yet. But Cheez knew he couldn't go against the grain. If his wife told her father, that's just how it would look to him. The only thing to do was to kill her or be killed.

* * *

Mr. and Mrs. Word were Trigga's first and longest tenants. He knew that their house was old and in need of repair, but the Words didn't sweat him about it. So to show his appreciation, Trigga moved them to one of his newly remodeled homes on 48th and Stark. The area was much nicer than on 30th and Lloyd where he moved them from. He also paid them enough to refurnish their new home, because he needed the old house to look lived in for the meeting with Cheez.

After everything was set and ready to go, the four of them sat around getting high off the kush that ETO had given to Dream. They decided to play the board game Risk with Rahji to pass time and try to take their minds off what they knew had to be done.

When they got the call from ETO telling them that Cheez had made his way to the city, the four of them dropped Rahji off at Sam's cousin's daycare, where Sam and his men would be waiting for Crunch and his men to show up to take the baby.

* * *

Crunch took Bully with him to meet the boss at the airport. Once he was in Cheez's SUV, Crunch was told about the deal that was made with Leslie.

"So we just supposed to give this bitch 150 bands and trust that she is telling us the truth about this shit?" Crunch questioned, turning in his seat to face Cheez.

"Pretty much. Only we're not going to let her go until we have Rahji and Dream. Do you still have men watching that house?"

"Yep! Night and day. Nothing's changed. No one even stopped by."

"Well, we going to send them to pick up my daughter. Once they let us know they have her, then Leslie will tell us where to find that bitch Dream and her new friends."

"Just so you know, when we have the address, I want Leslie sent to the motel to pick up the rest of the money. But the only payment she's going to get is a bullet in the head from your men," Amilia added to their plan.

"Okay, alright! I can make that happen. But tell me this. If I put two of us at the motel and send the others to pick up the kid, that only leaves Amilia and us."

"So your point is?" Amilia questioned Bully.

"Ma'am, I'm saying we in these niggas' city, and don't know how many men they have behind them."

"I don't give a fuck how many of these soft, cheese-head niggas it is. If you're scared, kill yourself now so I won't have to do it later!" Crunch snapped, not liking what Bully was telling them.

For the rest of the ride, Crunch was on his cell phone dishing out orders that he had received from the boss.

* * *

"Hey, boo, can you get away? I'm trying to get some more of that good D you put on me the other night."

"Is that right? Where you at?"

"Yeah, I can still feel you. Nina's already there at the motel working, but it's my day off, so I'm free to do whatever."

"Let me free up so I can make this happen."

The men at the motel had switched places with the ones in the car who were watching the house, so they could go and hook back up with the girls. Little did they know this was all part of ETO's plan. His home girl Stacy had texted them saying she was bringing another friend because Nina had to take her son to the hospital. ETO had her send them a photo of a female from a magazine that he was reading, and just as he thought, the photo was to their liking. The fools set up the time and place.

* * *

Leslie was glad to be alone. She could barely hold her composure. Trigga was doing what he felt was best to end all of their troubles and constant running. She couldn't back out now. Her best friend's and god-daughter's lives depended on her going through with it.

"What could he do with all these people around?" she thought as she stood with her back to the wall of the KFC on Third and Wright Streets.

Leslie scanned the crowd at the Juneteenth Festival. This is where she was to meet Cheez. She wished she had a gun or something on her person to protect herself, but she knew he would have her patted down. She took comfort in knowing that if Cheez tried anything, Paper was hiding under a tarp in back of his Ford F-350 with its tailgate down and his scope trained on her every move. Leslie also knew that if the opportunity presented itself, Paper would end Cheez right then and there. She had seen it in his eyes as he screwed a suppressor to the gun.

"Hello?" she answered the ringing of the Bluetooth in her ear.

"Les, look down. Do you see that cup in front of you in the street?"

"Yeah, bae. I see it."

She picked it up and looked inside.

"If it's dry put the address in it and put it in the grass next to the street lamp. I don't want him to touch you," Paper said while watching her in his sights.

"Man, I ain't going to lie. I'm scared as hell!" she admitted to him as she did what he told her to do.

"That's good. If you wasn't, you might tip him off to us. But I got you. Remember, I'm in my truck with my good eye on you. If he tries anything, he's done. I promise I won't let anything happen to you."

Leslie took a quick look over her right shoulder.

"I know you won't."

Even though she believed him, the fear wouldn't let her go.

* * *

At the house on 30th, Dream and Trigga worked on their escape routes, and then they hid guns around the house outside just in case.

"I'm so fucking nervous."

Dream's hands were shaking as she rubbed her temples.

"Do you think Rahji is scared? What if she's scared?"

"Hey, you're tripping now! How can she be scared when she don't know what's going on? She's in good hands with Dana at the daycare; plus Sam and his niggas are down there with her. The princess is good."

Trigga walked over and pulled her into his arms.

"It's going to be okay. Trust me. Can you do that?"

"Yes, I can trust you," she replied in between kissing and sucking on his neck.

"You know you about to get something started doing that!"

"That's what I'm trying to do."

She kissed him again.

"I need this right now to ease my mind," Dream told him while kicking off her shoes and then wiggling out of her pants.

"This shit's crazy!"

Trigga unbuckled his jeans and then bent her over the arm of the couch, giving in to her request.

Chapter 26

It's Show Time

Betrayal was natural in Cheez's world, and so was cold-blooded murder. He doubted that Leslie needed the money for real, because of the cash that Dream had taken when she made her run. But he also knew that money would make a person turn on their family.

Amilia glanced at the GPS when it said they had made it to the address Leslie had given them.

"Babe, let me take the money to her?"

"No! I'm not going to do that, Amilia!" Cheez answered firmly.

"Listen, she won't feel very threatened by another woman meeting with her, but if she sees you or one of your goons, she might get cold feet and run off. Why do

161

you think she picked a place with so many people around?"

"You right. But if anything happens to you, all of these cheese-head muthafuckers are going to die today."

"I would expect nothing less!"

Amilia kissed him, grabbed the cash, and then got out of the SUV.

When she was far enough away, Crunch ordered Bully to follow her from the other side of the street.

"If you think anything is out of place, grab her and then drag her back here if you have to!"

He took the words right out of his boss's mouth. Crunch knew how important Amilia's safety was to all of their lives.

As she pushed her way through the crowd of families and friends trying to enjoy the activities of the event, Amilia spotted who she believed to be Leslie. She had only seen her in photos from the few times she had Dream followed in the past. But Amilia was pretty sure it was the right woman who she was approaching.

"You must be Leslie?" Amilia asked, stopping right in front of her but still standing in the street at the curb.

"Who the hell are you?"

"You don't need to know that. All you need to know is this is for you as long as you got something for me?"

"I don't know you. Give me the bag first. I need to see the money because I don't trust none of y'all grimy muthafuckas!" Leslie told her while scanning the surroundings for a trap.

Amilia tossed the bag onto the ground in front of Leslie and then took a few steps back. When Leslie picked it up and looked inside and saw what she wanted, Amilia moved closer toward her.

"You better be careful now, because you might get robbed for your newfound riches."

"I ain't worried about it. The address is in that cup right there."

Leslie pointed at the cup and began to slowly back away.

"Hold up! We are going to be spending a little more time together until my people have the kid."

Amilia picked up the address and then quickly grabbed Leslie by the wrist.

"What? The address is real!"

"Then you don't have anything to worry about, do you?" Amilia explained as she pulled out her phone and called her husband.

Paper told Leslie to relax just to remind her that he was still there with her.

"I don't see him nowhere, but I got one of his guys watching you from across the street on your left. Don't look at him. I got it. You just focus on her," Paper explained to her while taking aim at Bully.

"Amilia, what's going on?" Cheez asked as soon as he answered.

"I'm doing my job. Here! Write down this address so they can go pick up our child."

Amilia made sure Leslie was hanging on her every word, so she knew just who she was dealing with.

"I knew I should not have let you go over there by yourself. Give me the address and get back here!"

"Not until I know they got her," Amilia responded, before she read Cheez the address.

After she heard him repeat it to Crunch, who sent their goons to pick up Rahji, she then hung up on him.

"Me staying here wasn't part of the deal that I made with Cheez," Leslie reminded her.

"Yeah, well I'm not him. So if you want the rest of the money, you'll wait."

"I'll wait for ten minutes, but I noticed you didn't give him the other address, where he could find his baby mama. I don't care what you're on, but I'll be needing the rest of my money if you got it, Amilia."

She repeated what Paper had told her to say, adding a few of her own words and letting Amilia know that she knew just who she was.

The two stood sizing each other up for a second while waiting for Cheez to let Amilia know they had his kid.

"Since you know who I am, you should know that this isn't going to end well for that bitch Dream once we get the baby."

"Not my concern. I just want my money!" Leslie lied while biting the inside of her lower lip to mask her anger.

"Well, you'll have to go get the rest of it from the motel after my husband calls to let me know that everything's good."

* * *

Mike and Ty pulled up in front of the daycare center, and both of them got out of their Jeep. Mike stayed outside and let Ty go in alone to pick up Rahji. Neither of them thought it took two to retrieve a small child from the center. Mike was a bit upset that he wasn't where the action was going to be.

"Hello, are you a parent or are you looking to enroll a child here? We have openings right now."

"No, I'm here to pick up Rahji," Ty told the pretty Angie Stone look-alike sitting at the front desk.

Dana's heart skipped at the sound of his request.

"Okay, I'm going to need you to sign her out and to see your ID."

"Shit! I don't have my ID on me," he said as he flashed her his best smile.

"No ID, no child. I'm sorry, but I have to record who I give these folks' children to," she informed him, before she returned the fake smile and then pretended to look something up on her computer.

"I understand. Will you accept getting the okay over the phone?"

"As long as it's one of the contacts I have here for her."

"Okay, let me make a call."

"Go right ahead."

Dana crossed her arms across her chest trying to hide her nervousness. She knew this was the guy who she was waiting for to attempt to pick up Rahji.

Ty walked away from the desk and made the call.

"Man, this bitch here is telling me that I need an ID to pick the kid up!" he explained to Crunch while standing in the doorway of the daycare.

"Cheez, Ty said they won't give her to him without showing ID, so what you want him to do?" Crunch asked.

Cheez knew the men didn't carry ID on them unless they were ordered to.

"Hold on! Amilia, tell that bitch you're with to call and tell them to give my daughter to Tyrone. He's there right now."

Amilia did as she was told, and Leslie pretended to call the daycare. However, in reality, Paper was on a three-way with Sam checking to see if things were ready on his end.

"Hey, Dana, this is Leslie. Is there someone there by the name of Tyrone to pick up Rahji?"

"Yeah, he just went outside to call somebody, but he didn't tell me his name." Dana stood up and walked over to the window. "There are only two of them that I can see."

"Okay! When he comes back, it's okay for Sam to give her to him."

"Alright!" Dana agreed, obviously reading between the lines.

Shortly after Dana ended the call with Leslie, Ty walked back inside.

"Is everything alright now?"

"Yes! I just got off the phone with her auntie. But you still have to sign her out."

She spun a clipboard in front of him.

"Name right here, please?" Dana pointed to a line next to Rahji's name.

Ty did as she asked and signed a fake name. Dana looked at it before she disappeared into the back to get the child and let her cousin in the back door.

168

When Dana was out of earshot, Ty called Crunch back.

"The fat bitch went to go get the kid now."

"Alright! Let me know when you got her."

Sam crept along the wall keeping his body close so he wouldn't be seen. Once he got close enough, he pulled out his gun and gave Dana the okay to take Rahji out to him. Sam reminded her to stick to the plan before she went. Outside, Little and E-Bay prepared to ambush Mike at the Jeep.

"I got her!" Ty informed Crunch, when he saw Dana walk around the corner with the child beside her.

"Alright, take her back to the room, and then meet us at the address I send to your phone," Crunch ordered before he ended the call and texted Ty the address.

"We got her, so I'll be seeing you around, sexy, "Amilia said to Leslie.

"Bye, baby!"

Leslie turned and quickly walked to the back door of the KFC restaurant, where the manager let her in. Paper had paid the man $200 to help make Leslie disappear safely.

"I'm in KFC," she informed Paper.

"Okay, stay there."

Paper continued to watch Amilia until she walked back to the SUV and got in. He couldn't make out the faces to see if Cheez was inside with her. Paper thought of just shooting the two men in the front seat just because, but he didn't want to mess up his chance at getting the person who killed his mother. He wanted to look the person in his eyes when he killed him, so the punk knew who killed him and why he died.

Chapter 27

Showtime

Hey, sweety, I almost forgot to give you your snack like I said I would. Come on, so you can pick out what you want."

"Okay, can I have a Rice Krispies Treat?"

"You sure can, and something else." Dana looked at Ty. "I'm sorry, we'll be right back. I promised her."

"It's okay. Go ahead, I got time," he told them as he shoved his hands inside his back pockets.

Dana rushed Rahji and the others into the infant room like they had practiced earlier that day. She chose this room because it didn't have windows low enough to climb through from the outside and there was only one way in. Shortly after they were all safely in the room with the door locked, Dana heard the first of many gunshots coming from outside.

The sound of gunfire made Ty pull out his gun and rush to the door to have a look at what was going on. He knew from the look of the area that it wasn't something that went on every night like in other parts of the city.

"Say, muthafucka, you should've taken off when you had the chance!" Sam explained.

Before Ty could make a complete turn and aim his gun, Sam shot him twice in the chest. When he dropped, he walked over to the dying man and kicked his gun out of reach.

"Dana!" Sam called out.

She rushed back to the desk area when Sam began calling her name.

"Here! Call the police just like we talked about."

Sam had shot Ty with a gun that was registered to her, so it wouldn't be much of an issue when she said that she feared for her life and the safety of the children in her care.

"9-1-1. Can I help you?"

"I—I need the police. A man with a gun tried to take one of my kids and I shot him," Dana explained to the operator.

"Okay, ma'am, someone is on the way. Is anyone else hurt?"

"No. I have all the children in the back room so they won't see this."

"Ma'am, can you tell me if the man you shot is breathing or not. Do you know where you shot him?"

"I—I don't know. I don't want to go by him."

"Okay, I understand. I need you to stay on the line with me in case we need a few more details."

"Alright!" Dana agreed.

She watched as Sam pulled out another gun and rushed outside to check on his men once the gunfire outdoors had stopped. He promised Dana he would stay with her until it was over, so she wasn't afraid.

* * *

Stacy knocked on the door, and Misty did her best not to look so nervous.

"Hey, papi!" Stacy greeted him when the door opened.

"What's good, ma. This must be the owner of that sexy hot shot you sent us?" Buck asked, after allowing the girls in the room.

"Did you like it?" Misty flirted and ran her long fingernails down his cheek.

"All I need to know is if it's as good as it looks on the phone?"

"Hey, where's Rob?" Stacy asked, getting right to the real job they were sent there to do, which was to find out how many men were in the room.

"Here I am, ma!" he replied, after walking in from the bathroom.

"I thought you stood me up or something when I didn't see you. I think my heart broke a little."

She gave him her sexy pouty face.

"Shit! I think I left my window down on my car," she said as she walked back to the door and unlocked it.

"While you're over there, you may as well hang the Do Not Disturb sign just in case one of the others comes back," Buck suggested as he groped Misty's butt.

Moments after Stacy closed the door, ETO burst in and fired a shot into the bed.

"Put your hands up so we can see them!" he ordered, taking aim at Rob as the rest of his goons rushed in the room behind him.

Buck couldn't believe what was happening and stupidly tried ETO by reaching for a gun lying on the table behind Misty. Instantly, ETO and one of his goon's triggers went to work, with every shot hitting home. With both men dead, the girls took the valuables from the room before they all rushed away from the scene.

ETO called Trigga once they were all safely out of the area.

"It's done, my nigga! That shit there was fun. You sure you don't need my help eating the beef over there?"

"I got it from here, E. I'll call you when the show is over."

"Make sure you do that! Love, my nigga!" ETO said before he ended the call.

"Let's swing over on 30th and Lloyd so I can watch them niggas put in work. Who knows! We might get some more action," he told his driver.

Chapter 28

Payback

Crunch repeatedly called his men at the motel, alternating both of their phones.

"Come on, this ain't the time to be fucking with them punk bitches!" he said quietly to himself.

Bully circled the block in both directions before pulling in front of the address that Leslie had given them. They were also following the GPS tracker that Amilia had slipped into the pocket of the gym bag holding the money that she gave to Leslie.

Cheez wasn't a fool. He knew that the dimly lit, run-down block was not Trigga's home address. The fact that it was pretty much deserted didn't escape him either.

"Amilia, stay in the fucking car. Let us handle this, so we can get out of this dump!"

The look in his eyes told her that he was serious, and it turned her on to see him act this way. Amilia agreed to let the three of them go on their own while she continued to scan the surroundings for a trap.

* * *

Trigga's good friend pulled onto the block just in time to witness Cheez and his men making their move on the house.

"Hey, go get that killa running around the back!" he ordered his men in the car in front of him. "Let's go wrap these fools up for my niggas. They'll get over it if they feel some type of way about me stepping in," he explained as he led four of his goons out of the big Suburban—all of them with their guns ready.

A pit bull ran from the darkness with its leash trailing behind him, but there was no master in sight. The men watched it run up the block. Cheez glanced over at his wife, who was watching them from the SUV.

"Slow up there. I wouldn't take another step if y'all are smart!" ETO said with his Glock aimed at Bully's head.

"Yeah, let us get them burners up off you," one of ETO's goons demanded.

Another one of his men walked up and took them right out of their hands.

"Look, you don't want to rob us!" Crunch said, giving up his gun without a fight, knowing he had another in his waist.

ETO pulled out his phone and called Trigga.

"Rob you? Ha! You funny," he laughed.

"Say, Trig. I know you told me you were good, but you know me. I'm young, rich, and hard-headed."

"E, what the hell are you talking about?" Trigga asked, when he answered his phone while watching the girls pass the time counting the cash that Cheez had paid Leslie.

"I'm outside, and I got a little something for you. So stop jackin' and come out here."

Trigga looked out the window next to the front door.

"Here we come!"

ETO ended the call.

"Bro, let's go see what E got going on for us outside."

Curiosity was the only reason Dream and Leslie followed them out the door. They could hear Cheez's voice out on the porch.

"If you and your boys walk away now, I'll make it worth it for you. Do you know who I am?" Cheez tried to bargain with the men holding them at gunpoint.

"Yeah, I know you. You something like a dead man talking," ETO said before he shut up Cheez with a smack of the gun he had taken from him.

Dream saw that ETO had Cheez, Crunch, and Bully lined up in the abandoned lot next to the house.

"Oh shit! Oh shit!"

"Dream! Dream! Calm the fuck down! He can't hurt us!" Leslie told her, taking her hand to let her know she wasn't alone.

Amilia was ducked down in the back of the Jeep. She had a gun that one of the men had left behind, but she wasn't foolish enough to try to go up against the gang in front of her that all had guns of their own. She knew it would be crazy to try to help them on her own, so she called the police and stayed put until they came to the rescue. For the first time, she feared for her husband and his men, and she shed tears as she prayed for them.

"Oh shit, it's my nigga Cheez!" Trigga joked as he showed his delight. "E, it's not my b-day, is it? I'm saying right now it feels like it."

Paper didn't see the need in holding back any longer. He walked up and started beating Bully with his gun.

"Which one of you bitch-ass niggas killed my mother?" he asked, breathing hard with his foot against Bully's chest while holding him to the ground.

Bully could see his own blood dripping from Paper's gun.

"Fuck you and that old bitch! I should've let them fuck her first, you bitch-ass nigga!" Crunch yelled as he rushed Paper for the gun.

He was met by two hard, strong haymakers. The first blow with gun in hand knocked Crunch to the ground, while the next returned quickly to strike him repeatedly, before Paper shot him point blank in the face.

"Paper! Paper! You good, bro?" Trigga asked.

He was a bit taken aback by the beating he witnessed.

"No!" Paper answered him, before he shot Crunch five more times in the chest. "But I am now!"

Paper then took hold of Leslie's hand to ground himself.

"I'll let you take care of this fool on your own."

Amilia had to look up from her hiding space when she heard all of the shots. Her heart was able to beat again once she saw that her man was still standing. Not knowing anything else to do, she called her father and told him what was going on. Mr. Gomez got right on it. He told her to stay hidden until the police got there, and he assured her that help was on the way.

"Why don't you show the bitch how much you care, and fight me man to man? Put the guns down and let's bring the '80s back!" Cheez challenged Trigga.

"Is that what you really want?"

"No. Shoot that muthafucka, Trigga! Don't fight him. That's what he do!" Dream pleaded.

"Ain't no honor in shooting an unarmed man, or do you got bitch in you like your man?"

Paper aimed his gun at Cheez's head.

"I'll show you bitch, nigga."

"Bro, you promised me this nigga. Let me handle this. I got it; and if I don't, then you know what to do," Trigga reminded Paper, who then lowered his gun.

They let Cheez up off his knees and gave them room to move around.

"Son, may the force be with you!" ETO joked. "Here, hit this shit right here. On second thought, I'll save you some, my nigga. This shit here will put you on your ass. Then your girl will be mad at me and shit."

"Hey, E!" He turned toward Dream's voice. "Shut the fuck up and get over here."

"Hey! Hey! Hey! You ain't been 'round long enough to be my mom!" he continued to joke as he stepped out of the way and passed the blunt to the closest person to him.

Cheez moved with lighting speed, sweeping Trigga off his feet, which made him fall to the ground. Cheez then tried to stomp him, but Trigga rolled out of the way and grabbed Cheez's leg. He then pulled it and twisted it in one motion, causing Cheez to stumble. Trigga jumped back up to his feet and dodged a kick. He hit Cheez on the chin, causing him to stagger again, but he didn't fall. Cheez moved fast, but a roundhouse kick to his side slowed him down. He grunted in pain as he staggered. Trigga went in on him, hitting him with a combination of blows and ending with a spinning back fist to the jaw. The sound of breaking bone was loud and clear as Cheez fell to the ground knocked out cold.

Out of nowhere a police car raced up and slammed on its breaks. The car shot its spotlight in their direction.

"Everybody stay where you are!" the cop demanded over the bullhorn.

Hearing the police's instruction made Amilia show herself.

"Mama, the police are here now. Tell Papa to hurry."

Once Mrs. Gomez was told what was going on, she refused to get off the phone with her daughter.

"Thank God, baby!"

No sooner than the praise left her lips did she hear the sound of gunfire.

"Oh my goodness! What was that? Are you okay?"

Amilia had just locked eyes with her husband's lover as she took a gun from the guy next to her and started shooting at the police car. Amilia dropped her phone as the car pulled out of harm's way, leaving Cheez in the midst of it. She was off and running before her mind could catch up to her feet. She sent shots at the fleeing crowd, with two of her wild gunshots hitting Stacy and killing her on the spot. A third hit Dream high in her back. Once Amilia made it to Cheez, she stopped firing and dragged him back to the Jeep. She picked up her cell phone before getting behind the wheel and speeding off. Mr. Gomez then ordered her to head straight to the airport.

"Mama, tell Papa to have the plane ready, and somebody that can help me."

"Okay, baby. It's already done. Is he alright?"

"He alive but knocked out. They beat him up bad, and I think he got shot. He's bleeding pretty bad. There's a lot of blood," Amilia explained in a bit of a panic.

"Do you know how to get to the airport?" her mother asked.

"I'm following the GPS, so I should get there okay. Mama, I got to get off so I can concentrate."

Her mother let her off the line, and she made it to the airport shortly after. There, the pilot helped her get Cheez on board.

Chapter 29

The Aftermath

Trigga braced himself against the front seat of the big SUV as his friend broke through the traffic while trying to make it to the hospital. Leslie held Dream's head in her lap as he kept pressure on the hole in her shoulder. The fact that Dream was lying there unconscious on the seat between them made them worry even more.

Trigga's heart almost stopped when he saw Dream get shot and drop to the ground. Right away he wished he would have just killed Cheez instead of playing with him first. Paper finally made it to the hospital. Trigga carried Dream through the emergency room door. As soon as the hospital staff saw them, they rushed to help him lay

Dream on a gurney. They didn't waste time asking questions; they took her right to an operating room.

"Leslie, you and bro go pick up Rahji and take her home. Don't bring her here. She don't need to see her mother like this. I'll stay here and keep y'all updated on what's going on," Trigga told Leslie in the waiting room.

Paper was parking his truck so they wouldn't have it towed away.

"Excuse me, but are you the one who brought in the woman who was shot?" a tired-looking officer asked.

Trigga casually walked away from Leslie so they wouldn't stop her from leaving. He mouthed her to go do as he said before addressing the officer.

"Yes, why? Is something wrong?"

"Well, it's the hospital's policy to inform the police when there is a shooting victim brought in the way you brought your friend in. I just have a few routine questions while we wait, if you don't mind?"

Trigga liked the way the officer tried to make it seem as if he had a choice.

"I understand, but I don't want to leave her here alone."

"We have a private waiting room for you and whatever family may come. The desk will send them to you so you can focus on your girl," the younger officer explained while never taking his hand far away from his gun.

Trigga knew he wasn't going to get out of this.

"Okay, lead the way!"

As he was being led through the secure doors, he saw Paper and Leslie rush through the front entrance.

* * *

Cheez sat at home with his wife and children, who were all doing their best to nurse him back to health. He suffered a few broken ribs, a broken jaw, and a gunshot to his right leg that Amilia thought she may have done when she was shooting at the others. The doorbell rang, and shortly after, a maid walked in followed by Mr. Gomez and two of his men.

"Hey, Grandpa!" the kids screamed excitedly as they ran up to give him hugs and kisses.

After giving in to his grandchildren's demands, he turned to his daughter.

"Princess, take the kids outside so I can speak to your husband alone."

"Papa, what is this sudden visit about?"

Amilia knew something was wrong and that her father was upset about the events that took place in Milwaukee. The visit worried her, because he never came to her home unannounced and without her mother.

"Don't question me, princess! Just do as you're told. This only concerns Cheez and myself. Now take them and run along."

She knew not to press the issue with him on her own, so she did as he told her and called her mother to try to find out what was going on.

"Mr. Gomez, I was going to call and thank you for getting me out of that city before I ended up in their prison," Cheez said as he stood up, shifting his weight from his bad leg with his cane.

Mr. Gomez slapped him hard in the face.

"I don't want your thanks! You think I came here for that or that I care for you? You're wrong. Punk, I trusted you with my business and, most importantly, my daughter. You put them both in jeopardy for what? A bitch?" The old man pushed him back into his seat.

"Sir, it's not like that. I'm not a fool, I—!"

"I didn't come here for your excuses either. I knew about your piece of ass and the kid from the start. Don't look surprised. I run this city, remember? I do not like you. Nothing goes on without me knowing before it happens. The only reason you're still breathing right now is because of my daughter, but she won't be able to save you the next time you fuck up. So if you're thinking of going after that bitch and kid again, I'll see to it you don't return. Are we clear?"

"Yes sir. I give you my word I'm done with it!"

"Tell my princess that her mother expects to see her this weekend, and, Cheez, I expect you to have replaced the men you lost by then as well. I'm leaving Secret here to keep an eye on things until you're back on your feet. He only answers to me, and he has orders to kill you if you do anything to put my family in harm's way again."

With that said, the ol' man coolly walked out of the house to his awaiting Town Car that returned him to the airport for his flight home.

Cheez steamed with anger. He didn't like having a watchdog, but he knew he had to play it cool with the old man. He lied when he said he was done with Dream. He would never let Dream have his child or let Trigga get away with what he had done to him. As soon as he could, Cheez planned to do just what Mr. Gomez told him to do. Rebuilding his crew was the first thing on his list. Only this time their only loyalty would be to him. Once that was done, he thought about killing the old man and anyone who was against him taking over the business.

"Babe, where's Papa? Is everything alright?" Amilia asked, snapping him out of his thoughts.

"He's gone, but everything's fine. He said your mother wants to see you and the kids this weekend."

"Yes, I know. I just got off the phone with her. I called her to try and find out why Dad was here."

"Did you?"

"No, she didn't know he was here. Tell me what's going on, and don't say nothing," Amilia demanded as she sat on the arm of the chair in which Cheez was sitting.

"It was just about business. He just wanted to be sure I was up to getting back on track, and to tell me he's leaving Secret here until I get back on my feet to help me get things back up and running. See, there's nothing for you to be concerned with," he explained to her, before he patted her on her butt.

"Okay if you say so!" she replied, before taking a sip of her drink.

Amilia smiled to herself at the thought of Secret being so close to her. She had been sleeping with him for almost a year. Every time she made a trip to Mexico, she found time to pleasure herself with her second love.

* * *

The Town Car pulled across from Mr. Gomez's plane on the private landing strip and stopped.

"You understand what I need you to do here?" he spoke for the first time since leaving his daughter's home.

"Yeah, you made it very clear back at the house," Secret answered with a chuckle, obviously still amused about the way Cheez got slapped by the boss.

"I think you should know that I've known about you and Amilia for a while now. Don't look surprised. It's part of the reason I chose you. But don't let your dick get in the way of doing your job. I want that good-for-nothing son-of-a-bitch dead, but you can't let Amilia know I'm behind it," Mr. Gomez explained, before he climbed out of the car.

Secret followed after stopping to tip the driver.

"Mr. Gomez, you don't have to worry about that. I'm here to do a job, and that's what I'm going to do. But it's going to take a little time to make it look like an accident. I'll hop right back on the next plane out once I'm packed."

"No! You stay here now. Anything you need, I'll have sent to you."

Mr. Gomez stopped at the steps of his plane and turned around.

"I have a private suite here. That's where you'll be staying. I'll have the doorman give you the keys when you get there. Only use the car. It was a gift I never liked from someone that's no longer with us. Get this done for me and this city is yours."

With that said, he turned and boarded the plane.

Secret got back in the Town Car, and the driver headed downtown to what would be Secret's future home, if he played his cards right. He couldn't hold back the widening smile as he thought of having everything that he dreamed of with the old man's blessings. His thoughts soon turned to ones of getting between Amilia's creamy thighs. He was looking forward to making that happen right under Cheez's weak little nose. Secret sat back and took in the site of the city that was very soon to be his.

Chapter 30

The Follow-Up

Dream awoke in a bedroom she never thought she would see again. When she saw the shattered mirror, pillows, and her makeup all over the floor, Dream did her best to suppress the urge to scream and cry. Instead she once again decided not to continue being a victim. She would fight until she couldn't anymore. As her feet touched the cold hardwood floor, Dream found a gun on the nightstand, and then she heard her daughter crying out for her.

The mother snatched up the gun and ran as hard as she could toward the sound of her baby girl's cries. When she made it into the main hall, Cheez was there standing a few feet in front of her with her daughter's hand gripped tightly in one of his dirty hands and the other extended out for her to come to him. As Dream took a step forward, Amilia came up from behind them covered in blood. As soon as she set eyes on Dream, a gun materialized in Amilia's hands. Dream then saw a bright flash as Amilia hatefully pulled the trigger.

The only pain that Dream felt was on the right side of her body, but she still forced her eyes open once again. This time she found herself in a hospital room in bed. The gunshots were coming from a television on the wall across the room. Trigga was sound asleep next to her in a chair.

"Trigga!"

Her voice was a dry whisper, which made her have to repeat herself.

"Yeah, yeah! Bae, are you alright?" he asked, snapping up quickly from his sleep at the sound of her voice.

"My body hurts, and my mouth is dry as hell."

Trigga handed her the warm apple juice from her breakfast tray and told her that she had gotten shot.

"Where's my baby?"

"She's at home with bro and Leslie."

"What happened?"

"Well, one of ETO's people was killed running next to you. My nigga E-Bay is down the hall. He was shot protecting Rahji at the daycare."

"What? What about Cheez?" Dream asked, wishing he was on the list of the dead.

"I don't know what's going on with him. When you started busting at the police and then got shot by Cheez's wife, I didn't care about nothing else but getting you help. But I've been watching the news since we got here, and they didn't say nothing about him."

Trigga kissed her.

"What was that for?"

"What? I can't kiss you now? That's fucked up!"

"No, I didn't mean it like that!"

She pulled him down and then kissed him again.

"I better call my baby and let her know I'm alright," she announced to Trigga after breaking their kiss.

"Dream, she don't know you're here. We didn't want to scare her. But you can call and let her hear your voice."

* * *

After the call, the doctor walked in.

196

"How's she doing?" he asked Trigga, before he noticed that Dream was awake.

"She's alive and cranky. Is there anything you can do about that, Doc?"

"No, buddy, I'm sorry. You're on your own with that."

They laughed as the doctor wrote on his clipboard.

"Hello, young lady. My name is Dr. Bleek. How do you feel this afternoon?"

"Like I want to get home to my baby."

"Well, let me check you over once more. If everything's all good and you can tell me that you're done getting yourself shot, I don't see why we should have to keep you," he answered, setting down his chart on the table.

The doctor then examined her bandages, and he explained to her that the bullet passed clean through. But the impact from it dislocated her shoulder, and the knot on her head was from the fall that knocked her unconscious.

* * *

Paper made all the necessary calls to keep Trigga out of jail as he took Leslie and Rahji home. When they got there, Rahji was asleep. Paper let Leslie take her to her room and put her down for bed while he found himself a much-needed drink. He took the bottle down to his bedroom. As soon as he walked through the door, his eyes fell on a photo of his mother, and tears of release slipped from his eyes before he blinked them away.

Leslie found Paper standing in the middle of his room with a drink in one hand and the other covering his face. She walked up and spun him around to her, wrapping her arms around his waist. Leslie first kissed his hand away, and then his tears as she made her way to his lips. All the while, she told him things were over now and everything would get better.

Leslie started undoing the buttons on his jeans while he pulled off his shirt. She pushed his jeans to the floor, and then pulled his hardness from its home in his boxers. Leslie raised her lips to his before dropping down and taking him in her mouth. She blew him until she tasted his release. She pulled back after taking his hardness in her hand and then milked him. Paper was still hard and ready for the next round. He picked her up off the floor, and she wrapped her long legs around his waist as he sucked on her neck. He carried her over to the bed, where he tossed her down.

Paper undid her jeans and snatched them off along with her boy shorts. As much as he wanted to be inside her, he took the time to taste her swollen mound. As his mouth worked its magic on her, she began to shiver and cum, drenching the bed and his chin. Unable to hold back any longer, Paper pulled her to the edge of the bed, flipping her over and pulling her on her knees before sliding deep up in her from behind. He pounded her hard and relentlessly, until he exploded his second load deep inside her wetness.

Afterward, the two lay holding tightly to one another, both thinking about their future and the well-being of their friends. After some time, the two fell asleep and were awakened by Dream calling to talk to her friend and daughter.

Chapter 31

The End?

Secret soon found his task of getting rid of Cheez to be an easy one. He couldn't believe how predictable he was. For the past week, Cheez ended his day at a strip club before he called it a night. The men he hired to replace the ones that were killed in Milwaukee were low-life wanna-bes that would do pretty much anything for a buck. Secret used this to his advantage. First, he weeded out the killers from the weak by offering them more money and an upper-level spot in his new organization. Once he had his team of three—Raymond, Dago, and Browny—he had them convince the others not to tag along with them to the strip club. They went along with it for the $500 he gave them. Only one refused to leave Cheez's side until he was home for the night. He made his choice to unknowingly die with Cheez.

Secret told Cheez that he had something to take care of, so Cheez dropped him back off at the Acura NSX that Mr. Gomez had given him. Secret always left the car parked at Cheez's home and rode with him, so this gave him the chance he was looking for to be alone with Amilia.

"Secret, do you think it's safe to be doing this here? What if—?"

"Shut up and trust me! Do you trust me, Amilia?" he asked, closing the distance between them.

"Yes, I trust you." Amilia took his hand. "Follow me, and let me show you just how much."

Amilia led Secret into a guest bedroom that was simply decorated and easy for her to clean quickly when they were done. When they were safely behind closed doors, Amilia let the sundress she was wearing fall to the floor, showing him her curvy birthday suit, hot for his touch.

"I've been thinking of being with you every second of the day since I got here. I need you, Amilia. You know you want me as much as I do you."

She unbuttoned his shirt to expose his toned bronze body. She loved his size. She kissed and sucked on his hard chest as her hands worked on getting him out of his pants.

"Baby, I told you if there was a way for us to be together, I would take it. If it's truly meant to be, I know God will make it happen for us." Amilia kissed her way onto her knees as he stepped out of his pants. "Let's just enjoy this until our time comes."

This was all Secret really wanted to hear before he got his job done.

"Okay, love. Let me," he said as he dropped down to her and quickly filled her mouth with his tongue in a deep passionate kiss.

"Oh, Secret. I want you inside me! I need you in me!" she begged as he sucked on her full breast.

"Shush! I know what you need," he told her, before he then dipped his head between her legs, sucking her inner thighs as he made his way to her sweet spot.

She was so hot and wet that it didn't take long for her to cum for him. Secret made his way back to her lips, letting Amilia taste her juices on his lips before he rolled her on top of him, picked her up, and lowered her down on his hardness. As his thickness filled her, she came a little more.

Amilia rode him hard, giving Secret every inch of her wetness. She dug her nails into his chest as his hardness began to swell and jerk in her. She knew he was about to bust, and she wanted to cum with him. So she slammed herself down harder and harder until she felt her passion release along with his.

"Wow! You really did miss me, didn't you?" Secret asked her while holding her shaking and sweaty body tight to his.

"Always!" was all Amilia could get out as she tried to catch her breath.

After a few moments, Secret rolled her off of him.

"I hate to go. But if I don't, Cheez will wonder where I am."

"I understand. Just promise me that we will do this again soon."

"I'm already thinking how I'm going to make that happen."

"You better take a shower before you go. You can use the one in here. I would get in with you, but that would be pushing it."

A half hour later, Secret was pulling up to the strip club. He let them direct him to where they wanted him to park. The club was full that night. Secret wondered what was so special about the night. He adjusted his gun, walked back to the entrance, and paid the $10 cover plus a tip to skip the line and pat-down. As soon as he walked in, a familiar waitress rushed over to escort him to the VIP booth where Cheez was waiting for him. Secret ordered a bottle and tipped her before she rushed off to get his order.

"I was starting to think you weren't going to make it," Cheez said, not taking his eyes off the big-titted beauty on stage. "So, when do I get to meet her?"

"Why do you think I was with a woman?"

"Well, you don't come off as someone that likes men, and you look like you just stepped out of a shower."

Secret made a note to himself to give himself more time to get his act together before going out with Cheez after being with Amilia. But if things went as planned, he wouldn't have to worry after tonight.

"She's just some ass. Nobody I want to be down with like that."

"Be careful with that. Remember, that's pretty much how I got in the mess I'm in with the old man now!" Cheez laughed, even though he wasn't joking one bit.

The DJ announced a new girl to the stage and the club went wild. Both men and women rushed the stage as the song started and the country-thick caramel beauty charged onto the runway. The crowd didn't waste time showing her their love as cash was thrown at her from all sides of the stage. Secret watched how excited Cheez was about her as well. He shook his head at how Cheez was standing up in his seat for this show when he had something much better at home.

Browny made eye contact with Secret, and then waved his phone in the air for Secret to take a look at his. On it was a text from Raymond telling him to move away now. Secret didn't ask any questions. He just got up and walked closer to the stage like he really wanted to see the girl up closer.

"Yeah, that's what I'm talking about. See if you can get that bitch to leave with us!" Cheez yelled behind him.

On the far side of the club, Raymond started a fight with Dago, who pulled his gun and sent shots into the mirrors behind the bar. He deliberately missed Raymond to make things look good. The club went wild with people rushing to get to the door or to take cover.

Browny ran over to Cheez at the booth and half-carried him away from the sounds of the gunshots. The goon who still worked for Cheez pulled out his gun and followed closely behind them, but he didn't watch his own back. Secret ran up and fired two shots into the side of his chest. Cheez turned and looked back to see it happen, but he wasn't fast enough to stop Browny from slamming him to the ground and then shooting him a few times in his chest.

Secret walked over and bent down to whisper into the dying man's ear.

"Punk, I just took your life. Everything you had is now mine, even your wife."

He smiled as he shot Cheez once more in the head before falling in with the crowd and getting away.

* * *

"So what are your plans now that this shit with Cheez is done with or whatever?" Trigga asked while helping Dream get into his Magnum.

"What do you mean, what am I going to do? That nigga could come back looking for me again at any time. I ain't no fool! I'm going to stay in the safest place I know for me and family."

"So where is that?"

"With you and Paper. I ain't ever felt this safe in my life. So you stuck with us, boo," she answered with a nervous smile.

"What about Leslie, how do you know she wants to stay?"

"She's good. Paper got her. She let him get in the car. I'm glad she found love in him, so maybe I can be an auntie one of these days," Dream said with a laugh before grunting in pain.

"You okay?"

"Yeah, I can't be doing too much laughing right now."

Trigga leaned over and kissed her.

"I like your choice. I think I love you!"

"What you mean you think? You don't know?" she asked, pulling back from his lips.

"No, I don't." He pulled out of the parking lot. "I never been in love before, so this is new to me. But since you're staying, I hope you can teach me?"

"In that case, I think I love you too. Now we can learn together."

Dream closed her eyes and gave thanks to the Lord for answering all her prayers and placing her where she needed to be to live the life she had only dreamed of.

Text Good2Go at 31996 to receive new release updates via text message.

Please leave your review the author needs your support

To order books, please fill out the order form below:

To order films please go to **www.good2gofilms.com**

Name:_____

Address:_____

City:_____ State:_____ Zip Code:_____

_____

Phone:_____

Email:_____

Method of Payment: Check VISA MASTERCARD

Credit Card#:_____

Name as it appears on card: _____

Signature: _____

Item Name	Price	Qty	Amount
48 Hours to Die – Silk White	$14.99		
A Hustler's Dream - Ernest Morris	$14.99		
A Hustler's Dream 2 - Ernest Morris	$14.99		
A Thug's Devotion – J.L.Rose & J.M.McMillon	$14.99		
Black Reign – Ernest Morris	$14.99		
Bloody Mayhem Down South	$14.99		
Business Is Business – Silk White	$14.99		
Business Is Business 2 – Silk White	$14.99		
Business Is Business 3 – Silk White	$14.99		
Childhood Sweethearts – Jacob Spears	$14.99		
Childhood Sweethearts 2 – Jacob Spears	$14.99		
Childhood Sweethearts 3 - Jacob Spears	$14.99		
Childhood Sweethearts 4 - Jacob Spears	$14.99		
Connected To The Plug – Dwan Marquis Williams	$14.99		
Connected To The Plug 2 – Dwan Marquis Williams	$14.99		

Connected To The Plug 3 – Dwan Williams	$14.99		
Deadly Reunion – Ernest Morris	$14.99		
Flipping Numbers – Ernest Morris	$14.99		
Flipping Numbers 2 – Ernest Morris	$14.99		
He Loves Me, He Loves You Not - Mychea	$14.99		
He Loves Me, He Loves You Not 2 - Mychea	$14.99		
He Loves Me, He Loves You Not 3 - Mychea	$14.99		
He Loves Me, He Loves You Not 4 – Mychea	$14.99		
He Loves Me, He Loves You Not 5 – Mychea	$14.99		
Lord of My Land – Jay Morrison	$14.99		
Lost and Turned Out – Ernest Morris	$14.99		
Married To Da Streets – Silk White	$14.99		
M.E.R.C. - Make Every Rep Count Health and Fitness	$14.99		
Money Make Me Cum – Ernest Morris	$14.99		
My Besties – Asia Hill	$14.99		
My Besties 2 – Asia Hill	$14.99		
My Besties 3 – Asia Hill	$14.99		
My Besties 4 – Asia Hill	$14.99		
My Boyfriend's Wife - Mychea	$14.99		
My Boyfriend's Wife 2 – Mychea	$14.99		
My Brothers Envy – J. L. Rose	$14.99		
My Brothers Envy 2 – J. L. Rose	$14.99		
My Brothers Envy 3 – J. L. Rose	$14.99		
Naughty Housewives – Ernest Morris	$14.99		
Naughty Housewives 2 – Ernest Morris	$14.99		

Naughty Housewives 3 – Ernest Morris	$14.99		
Naughty Housewives 4 – Ernest Morris	$14.99		
Never Be The Same – Silk White	$14.99		
Stranded – Silk White	$14.99		
Slumped – Jason Brent	$14.99		
Someone's Gonna Get It – Mychea	$14.99		
Summer's Dirty Little Secret – Ernest Morris	$14.99		
Supreme & Justice – Ernest Morris	$14.99		
Supreme & Justice 2 – Ernest Morris	$14.99		
Supreme & Justice 3 – Ernest Morris	$14.99		
Tears of a Hustler - Silk White	$14.99		
Tears of a Hustler 2 - Silk White	$14.99		
Tears of a Hustler 3 - Silk White	$14.99		
Tears of a Hustler 4- Silk White	$14.99		
Tears of a Hustler 5 – Silk White	$14.99		
Tears of a Hustler 6 – Silk White	$14.99		
The Panty Ripper - Reality Way	$14.99		
The Panty Ripper 3 – Reality Way	$14.99		
The Solution – Jay Morrison	$14.99		
The Teflon Queen – Silk White	$14.99		
The Teflon Queen 2 – Silk White	$14.99		
The Teflon Queen 3 – Silk White	$14.99		
The Teflon Queen 4 – Silk White	$14.99		
The Teflon Queen 5 – Silk White	$14.99		
The Teflon Queen 6 - Silk White	$14.99		

The Vacation – Silk White	$14.99		
Tied To A Boss - J.L. Rose	$14.99		
Tied To A Boss 2 - J.L. Rose	$14.99		
Tied To A Boss 3 - J.L. Rose	$14.99		
Tied To A Boss 4 - J.L. Rose	$14.99		
Tied To A Boss 5 - J.L. Rose	$14.99		
Time Is Money - Silk White	$14.99		
Two Mask One Heart – Jacob Spears and Trayvon Jackson	$14.99		
Two Mask One Heart 2 – Jacob Spears and Trayvon Jackson	$14.99		
Two Mask One Heart 3 – Jacob Spears and Trayvon Jackson	$14.99		
Wrong Place Wrong Time – Silk White	$14.99		
Young Goonz – Reality Way	$14.99		
Subtotal:			
Tax:			
Shipping (Free) U.S. Media Mail:			
Total:			

Make Checks Payable To:

Good2Go Publishing

7311 W Glass Lane

Laveen, AZ 85339

"Text Good2Go at 31996 to receive new release updates via text message."

05735 2404

CPSIA information can be obtained
at www.ICGtesting.com
Printed in the USA
LVHW08s0803061018
592633LV00016B/125/P

9 781947 340176